W.H.G. Kingston

The Loss of the Royal George

W.H.G. Kingston

The Loss of the Royal George

ISBN/EAN: 9783337086176

Printed in Europe, USA, Canada, Australia, Japan

Cover: Foto ©Andreas Hilbeck / pixelio.de

More available books at **www.hansebooks.com**

THE LOSS

OF THE

"ROYAL GEORGE"

BY

W. H. G. KINGSTON

AUTHOR OF
"PETER THE WHALER" "THE THREE MIDSHIPMEN"
"THREE LIEUTENANTS" "THE HEROIC WIFE"
ETC. ETC.

ILLUSTRATED BY H. W. PETHERICK

GRIFFITH FARRAN BROWNE & CO. LIMITED
35 BOW STREET, COVENT GARDEN
LONDON

THE LOSS OF THE "ROYAL GEORGE"

CHAPTER I

MY father, Richard Truscott, was boatswain of the *Royal George*, one of the finest ships in the navy. I lived with mother and several brothers and sisters at Gosport.

Father one day said to me, "Ben, you shall come with me, and we'll make a sailor of you. Maybe you'll some day walk the quarter-deck as an officer."

I did not want to go to sea, and I did not care about being an officer; indeed I had never thought about the matter, but I had no choice in it. I was but a very little chap, and liked playing at marbles, or "chuck penny," in our backyard, better than anything else.

"He is too small yet to be a sailor," said mother.

"He is big enough to be a powder-monkey," observed my father ; and as he was not a man who chose to be contradicted, he the next day took me aboard his ship, then fitting out in Portsmouth harbour, to carry the flag of Admiral Sir Edward Hawke. She was indeed a proud ship, with the tautest masts and the squarest yards of any ship in the British navy. She carried one hundred and four guns, all of brass—forty-two pounders on the lower deck ; thirty-two on the middle deck ; and twenty-four pounders on the quarter-deck, forecastle, poop, and main-deck. She had huge lanterns at her poop, into which four or five of us boys could stow ourselves away ; and from the time she was first launched, in 1756, the flag of some great admiral always floated from the masthead. When my father left me, to attend to his duty, I thought I should have been lost in the big ship, with deck above deck, and guns all alike one another on either side ; and hundreds of men bawling and shouting, and rushing about here and there and everywhere. Sitting down on a chest, outside his cabin,—my legs were not long enough to reach the deck,—I had a good cry ; and a number of boys, some of them not much bigger than myself, came and had a look at me, but they did not jeer, or play me any tricks, for they had found out that I was

the bo'sun's son, and that they had better not.   I
soon, however, recovered, and learned to find my way,
not only from one deck to another, but up aloft; and
before many days were over, had been up to the main-
truck; though when my father heard of it, for he was
below at the time, he told me not to go again till I was
bigger.   As I was continually, from ignorance, getting
into scrapes, and he could not keep an eye on me
himself, he gave me in charge to Jerry Dix, the one-
legged fiddler and cook's mate.   Jerry could take very
good care of me, but was less able to take care of
himself when he had got his grog aboard, and more
than once when this happened I had to watch over
him.   This made us firm friends, and I am very sure
that he had a sincere affection for me.

England was now engaged in what was known as
the Seven Years' War, which began in 1756, and had
been going on for three years, the ships of England
fighting those of France whenever they could find them,
and generally giving them a drubbing.   Our ship,
which carried, as I have said, the flag of Admiral Sir
Edward Hawke, had, with several other line-of-battle
ships, been for some time watching the French fleet,
under Admiral Conflans, shut up in Brest harbour,
when, a heavy gale coming on, we were obliged to put

into Torbay for shelter. We remained there for some time, while it blew great guns and small arms, which Jerry told me would keep the French ships shut up in harbour as securely as would our cannon. At length the weather moderated, and our admiral made the signal for the fleet to sail. It was a fine sight to see twenty-four line-of-battle ships, beside the *Royal George*, mostly seventy-four's, some larger and some smaller, getting under way together, and standing over to the enemy's coast. We were a few hours later than we should have been, however, for on our arrival we heard that Admiral Conflans had just before slipped out of Brest harbour, and sailed away for Quiberon Bay, hoping to cut off a small English squadron under Commodore Duff at anchor there.

We made all sail in chase, but a strong south-easterly wind blew in their teeth, and it was four days before we arrived off Belle Isle, when we were joined by Commodore Duff, with four fifty-gun ships and six frigates. Early in the morning, the *Maidstone*, one of our look-out frigates, made the signal that the enemy's fleet was in sight ! We, on this, threw out the signal for our ships to form in line, while the frigate was sent in-shore to ascertain how far we were from it. You will understand that the fog prevented

us from seeing the land or the enemy, and from the
same cause it was no easy matter, as we all sailed
close together, to prevent one ship from running into
another.

We had not long to wait, however, before, the fog
lifting, we caught sight of the French fleet, crowding
all sail to get away from us, for their frigates had found
out our fleet, while ours had discovered theirs. We
made all sail in chase, both the enemy's ships and ours
having every stitch of canvas they could carry. In
about three hours the van of our fleet got up with
them.

I remember standing by my father's side, in the
forecastle, and thinking what a grand sight it was,
as the *Warspite* and *Dorchester* gallantly commenced
firing their broadsides into the enemy. The next ship
that got into action was the *Magnanime*, commanded
by the brave Lord Howe, followed quickly by the
Revenge, *Torbay*, *Montagu*, and many others whose
names are known to fame. There was a heavy sea
running at the time, and, big as were our ships, they
kept tumbling about so much that we were unable to
fight our lower-deck guns. The captain of one of the
French ships, the *Thesée*, engaged with the *Torbay*,
thought that he could do so; and Captain Keppel,

who commanded the English seventy-four, unwisely
followed his example. The two ships were thus hotly
engaged, firing their broadsides into each other, when
we saw the Frenchman give a lurch to starboard, and
then down she went; out of all her gallant crew of
eight hundred men, only twenty being saved by the
British boats. The *Torbay* was very nearly following
her, but by great exertions the guns were run in, and
the ports closed, though not till she had shipped a good
deal of water.   Directly afterwards another Frenchman
sank before our eyes, as we guessed, from the same
cause.

I can't say that I saw much more of what took
place, for we were now going into action, and I was
sent below to attend to my duty, which was to bring
up ammunition in a tub, and to sit upon it on the
maindeck, with the other ship's boys, till it was
wanted to load the guns. We were soon thundering
away at the enemy, clouds of smoke filling the space
between the decks, through which I could dimly see
the crews of the guns, stripped to the waist, running
them in to load, and running them out again as
rapidly as they could. Shouts from the upper deck
reached us, and we heard that one of the French ships
had struck, but so heavy a sea was running, that no

boat could be lowered to take possession of her; several others were also severely handled, and one completely dismasted. Night was coming on; and as we were but a short distance from the shore, the admiral made a signal for the fleet to anchor, and we, rounding - to, brought up. There we lay, the wind roaring and the sea foaming and tossing around us, anxiously waiting for daylight. I had not seen my father, who was, as I supposed, at his station on the upper deck, when the order came to secure the guns. I was still sitting on my tub joking with the other boys, who were congratulating themselves at not being killed, when Jerry Dix came stumping along the deck towards me; he took my hand kindly, and I thought I saw him wipe away a tear from his eye.

"What is the matter, Jerry?" I asked, seeing that something was wrong.

"Ben, my boy, he that's gone told me to look after you, and so I will as long as I have a shot in the locker. You don't hear his pipe, do you? and you never will no more. There's the order to return powder to the magazine—as soon as you come up again, look out for me."

The other boys and I hurried below to the magazine

with our tubs; as soon as I came up I looked out for Jerry.

"What were you talking about?" I asked, having a feeling that something had happened to my father, though I scarcely dared to ask what.

"As I was saying, Ben, you have a friend in me if you have no other," said Jerry, again taking my hand. "You will grieve, my boy, I know, but it can't be helped; so I must out with it. We have not lost many men, but one has gone who was worth a dozen of the best; the Frenchman's round shot coming aboard took off his head, and deprived you of your father and us of our bo'sun."

"Do you mean to say that father's killed?" I asked in a trembling voice, unable to believe the fact.

"Yes, boy, he has sounded his last pipe; we shall no more hear his voice rousing up all hands, or hailing the maintop; but he died doing his duty. We could have better spared a worse man, but there is no help for it; and so, Ben, don't pipe your eye."

Notwithstanding Jerry's exhortations, I did, however, cry heartily as I lay in my hammock; and even the other boys respected my sorrow, though it did not last long, I must confess.

The next day was an exciting one. As the morning

broke, we saw our prize on shore, and another French ship at anchor dismasted; she, on seeing us, also ran on shore; when the *Essex*, a sixty-four, being sent in to take possession of her, was also wrecked; while another ship, the *Resolution*, seventy-four, was discovered on the rocks, the sea beating over her; and, before assistance could be sent, most of her gallant crew had perished. We succeeded, however, in burning the two French ships; but others, which were almost falling into our hands, by heaving their guns overboard, managed to escape up the river, where we could not follow.

"Although we have gained the victory, I do not see that we have gained much else for our trouble," observed Jerry, who was a philosopher in his way. "We have, you see, destroyed four French ships, and sent well-nigh two thousand Frenchmen, more or less, out of the world, but then we have lost two of our own ships and some hundred British seamen; and, worse than all, our brave bo'sun, your father."

The loss of my father was not to be repaired. I cannot say what might have happened had he lived, but losing him I grew up from boy to man, knocking about the world with many a chance of being knocked on the head, and yet with not the slightest hope of

ever treading the quarter-deck as an officer—not that I
ever thought about that. Jerry proved my firm friend.
Though fond of his grog, for my sake he kept sober,
that he might better look after me.

"Your father, Ben, lent me a helping hand when I
had not a shot in the locker and was well-nigh starv-
ing, and it's my duty to help you; and so I will, boy,
as long as I can keep my fiddle-stick moving, and get
a crust to put into my mouth."

Jerry did me an essential service, for having seen
better days he had got some learning, which was more
than most men in the ship possessed, and he taught
me to read and write, of which I knew nothing when I
came to sea. Even my father, though boatswain of a
line-of-battle ship, had not been much of a scholar.
However, I am not now going to write about myself
or my own adventures. When the ship was paid off,
as my poor mother could not support me, and I had no
fancy for any other calling, I went to sea again with
Jerry, who got the rating of cook's mate on board the
Thunderer, seventy-four.

I was now a stout lad, and could stand to my gun
or handle a cutlass as well as any man. We were
stationed off Cadiz, with three other smaller vessels,
looking out for a French squadron expected to sail for

that port. Being driven off the coast by bad weather, on our return we found that the Frenchmen had slipped out, so away we went under all the canvas we could set in pursuit. We had come in sight of the *Achille*, a sixty-four gun ship, and, soon getting up with her, we opened our broadside, receiving a pretty hot fire from her in return. We were blazing away at each other, when a noise louder than all our guns together sounded in my ears, and I felt myself lifted off my legs and shot along the deck. For the moment I thought the world had come to an end, or that the ship had blown up. On opening my eyes, I caught sight of a number of dead and wounded men lying around me, and the after-part of the ship in flames. Among them, seeing Jerry, I picked myself up and ran to him.

"Are you killed, Jerry?" I asked.

"No, it's only my wooden leg knocked away," he answered. "Just get me a mop-stick, or bit of a broken pike, and I shall soon be on my pins again."

Jerry having soon spliced a piece of the mop-stick which I brought him to the stump of his leg, I set him on his pins. Meantime I found that one of the quarter-deck guns, having burst had created the havoc I have described and set the ship on fire. All hands labouring away with buckets, we got the flames extinguished, and stood after the enemy, who was trying to escape. We again, however, came up with her; and running alongside, the boarders were called away, headed by our first lieutenant, Mr. Leslie, whom I followed closely. We had sprung on the deck of the enemy, and a big Frenchman was about to cut him down, when I caught the blow on my cutlass, and saved his life. One hundred and fifty gallant fellows coming on board after us, we quickly swept the Frenchmen from the deck, and they, crying out that they surrendered, we hauled down their flag. I did not think that Mr. Leslie was aware of the service I had rendered him till he thanked me for it, and ever afterwards was my friend. I had the good chance, also, some time afterwards, of keeping his head above water, when our ship, the *Laurel*, was capsized in a hurricane in the West Indies; and though, of course, it was what I would have done for anyone, I was very thankful to have been the means of again saving his life, though I ran, he always declared, no little risk of losing my own. I served with him when he commanded the *Favourite*, sloop-of-war, and afterwards in the *Active*, frigate, when we captured a Spanish galleon, which put some hundred pounds into the pockets of each of the men, and a good many thousands into those of the captain. I was pretty fortunate on board other ships, in which I sailed to different parts of the world, getting back to old England safe at last.

CHAPTER II

GETTING back safe home at last, like many another sailor, I might have sung—

> "'Twas in the good ship *Rover*
> I sail'd the world around,
> For full ten years and over
> I ne'er touch'd British ground.
> And when at length I landed,
> I could not long remain;
> Found all my friends were stranded,
> So went to sea again."

Jerry, the truest of them, who had at the Peace gone on shore, I could nowhere hear of; my poor mother was dead, my brothers at sea, and my sisters either married or in service. One of the youngest, my sister Jane, I was told was living near Ryde with the family of a captain in the navy, and on inquiry I found he was no other than my old commander, Captain Leslie. I started at once with my pockets pretty well lined with gold, for I had just received a good lumping share of prize-money, which I was sorely puzzled to know

18

what to do with. I was pleased at the thought of again seeing my old captain, though I scarcely fancied he would remember much about the little services I had done him. Who should open the door but Jane herself! She did not know me, but I knew her, though she had grown from a girl into a young woman, and I soon persuaded her who I was. She asked me down into the kitchen; and after we had had a talk, and she had told me all about those I cared for, she said she would go and tell Captain Leslie and his lady, who had often spoken to her about me, for they had found out that she was my sister. I was sent for into the drawing - room, when the captain welcomed me kindly, and told his wife and the young ladies—for there were two of them, besides a number of small children, boys and girls—how I had twice saved his life.

" I hope that you will stop as long as you like, and I will get you a lodging close at hand," he said in his pleasant way. " I have often wished that I could have shown my gratitude more than I have been able to do."

I told him not to trouble himself about that, as it was a pleasure to me to think that I had been of service; and as I had more money than I knew what

to do with, and never wished to be anything but what
I was, I didn't see how he could have done more than
he had done.

"I like your independent spirit, Ben," he said, "but
perhaps a time may come, when I may be able to serve
you as I should wish."

After a good talk of old times, I went back into the
kitchen. I had been sitting there for some time, when
a young woman came in with the sweetest face I ever
set eyes on. I got up and made a sort of bow, with a
scrape of my foot and a pull at a lovelock I wore in
those days, for it was not for me, I felt, to sit in the
presence of one like her; when Jane, laughing, said—

"Why, Ben, don't you know Susan Willis?"

She was one of a lot of little girls I remember living
next door to us, and I used to take her on my knee
and sing to her, and tell her about Lord Hawke and
the *Royal George,* when I was at home for the first
time after going to sea. Susan smiled, and put out her
hand, and that moment I felt I was not my own
master; her voice was as sweet as her smile, and had
the true ring of an honest heart in it.

"She is the young ladies' own maid," said Jane;
"and they are as fond of her as everyone is who
knows her."

"I am sure of it," says I; "and I am thankful that I am among them."

Susan looked down and blushed, and so I believe I did, though she could not see my blush through the brown skin of my face as well as I could see the rose on her lily cheeks.

Well, the long and the short of it is that day after day I went up to the house, and at last—I couldn't help it—I knew that I should be miserable if Susan wouldn't be mine, so I asked her to marry me. How my heart did beat when she said· yes. The captain and his lady were agreeable, and when they heard that I had a matter of three hundred pounds prize-money, or more, they observed that it was a prudent match; and so I took a cottage and furnished it, not far off, that Susan might go up and see Mrs. Leslie and the children whenever they wished, and we were married and were as happy as the day was long. I know I was, and Susan seemed contented with her lot.

Susan was a prudent young woman, and one day she says to me, "We must do something, Ben, to make a living."

"Why do you think that, Susan?" I asked; "I have got no end of prize-money."

"It's just this," says she; "you may think there is

no end, but it will come to an end, notwithstanding; what with the rent, and furnishing the house, and the new clothes you got me, and the weekly bills, we have spent fifty pounds of it already. Now, if we could set up a shop, or you could turn carpenter or gardener, or go into service with someone living hereabouts, we could lay up the rest of the money till a rainy day; and as we have a pretty spare room, I might take in a lodger to help out the rent."

I had never before thought of that sort of thing; but I was sure that Susan was right, and I began to turn in my mind what to do. I soon found that I was not fit for anything Susan proposed. I never was much of a carpenter, and I knew nothing about gardening. I tried my hand in my own garden, and had got everything shipshape as far as the palings, walks, and borders were concerned, but I could get nothing to come up. Still I kept thinking of Susan's remark, and, seeing the wisdom of it, I knew that there was only one thing I was fit for, and that was to go to sea. I was loath to part from Susan, but there was no help for it. There came about this time a hot press at Portsmouth; and as more than once the pressgangs had landed in the Isle of Wight, I was very sure that unless I got stowed away securely I should be picked up. Now, thinks I, it's better to enter as a free man; and hearing that my old ship, the *Royal George*, which was lying at Spithead, was in want of hands, after a talk with the captain and poor Susan, whose heart was well-nigh ready to break, though she could not help acknowledging that I was right, I went on board and entered. Captain Leslie had given me a note to Captain Waghorn, her commander, and I was at once rated as quartermaster. The flag of the brave Admiral Kempenfelt, who had a year before been appointed Admiral of the Blue, flew aboard her. We sailed shortly afterwards with a strong squadron for Brest, to look after a French fleet which had just left that port, conveying a large number of merchantmen bound for the East and West Indies. On the 12th of December we had the good fortune to discover the enemy's fleet about thirty-five leagues to the westward of Ushant, we being a long way to leeward of the convoy. I heard the admiral talking to the captain.

"We will cut off the merchantmen first, and fight the enemy afterwards," says he.

What he had determined on he was the man to carry out, and before evening we had picked up twenty merchantmen, laden with provisions and naval and military stores, two or three regiments of soldiers, and a large number of seamen. The *Royal George* had to heave-to for the rest of the squadron, which was a long way astern.

Next morning the French fleet was increased by a number of other ships appearing to leeward. The admiral was a prudent as well as a brave man, and considered that it would be wiser not to engage them, and so with our prizes we sailed back to Portsmouth. I could almost see my cottage from the maintop, but I could not get leave to go on shore; and as to having Susan off to see me, that I would not think of, for she would have had to see and hear things such as I did not wish my wife to witness. We again sailed for a cruise down Channel, and, after putting into Torbay, once more returned to Portsmouth. Admiral Kempenfelt, we had heard, had been appointed to the command of the fleet in the Mediterranean, and we expected to sail again in a week or less. This was in August 1782. Lord Howe's fleet was also lying off Spithead, among them the *Victory*, *Barfleur*, *Ocean*, and *Union*, all three-deckers, close to us, and numerous other men-of-war and merchant vessels; indeed, the people who came off from Portsmouth declared they could hardly see the Isle of Wight on account of the masts and spars of the ships. In consequence of going foreign we had been paid in golden guineas. As soon as I had received my pay, I got leave to go on shore to spend a couple of days, to be off again on the evening of the 27th. I had no difficulty in getting a boat, for there were hundreds pulling backwards and forwards. I found Susan bright and well, and looking out for me, for I had written to say I hoped to come. We went up to see Captain Leslie and the ladies, who had sent word that they wished us to pay them a visit. They were as kind as ever. The hours went by a great deal too fast.

A sailor's wife has a hard trial to bear, to have her husband at home for two or three days, and then away for as many years or more; however, I hoped to be at home again in less time than that, and so I cheered up Susan, and promised for her sake to take the best care of myself I could. She had not given up her notion of taking in a female lodger. We were standing in the porch of the cottage on the last day, when we saw a young lady in black, leading a little boy, coming along the road. The little chap had a sailor's hat and jacket on, though he did not seem much more than three years old.

"She is some officer's widow," I remarked to Susan as we watched her.

"She seems almost too young to be the mother of that child; she is his sister, more likely," answered Susan.

The young lady had stopped, and was looking about her; presently she came on to us.

"Can you tell me if I am likely to find a lodging hereabouts for a few days?" she asked in a sweet voice; " I have left my luggage at the inn in the village, but I do not wish to remain there, and I feel very tired with walking about."

"Will you like to walk in, miss, and rest yourself?" said Susan, "for you do look tired and ill too."

The young lady's cheek was very pale.

"I shall indeed be thankful if you will let me do so," she answered, and coming in she sank down in a chair.

Susan got tea ready; it seemed to revive her a little; the child, I observed, did not call her mother; and as I saw no wedding ring on her finger, I began to think that Susan was right about her not being the child's mother. Susan was evidently taken with the young lady, and, calling me out, she said that she would ask her to stop, as she did not seem fit to walk back to the village. I offered to go to the inn and fetch her things, but she had a bag in her hand which she said contained sufficient for the night, and she would send for them the next morning. I soon afterwards had to go off to the ship, so I saw no more of the young lady, who had gone to her room with the little boy.

CHAPTER III

WHAT a change it was from the quiet cottage, with my sweet Susan by my side, to the lower deck of the big ship, crowded with people, not only her own seamen and marines, but some hundreds of visitors, women and children! some of them the honest wives of the men, but others drunken, swearing, loud-talking creatures—a disgrace to their sex. Quarrelling and fighting and the wildest uproar were taking place; and then there were a number of Jews with pinchbeck watches, and all sorts of trumpery wares, which they were eager to exchange for poor Jack's golden guineas. Some of them went away in the evening, but many more came back the next morning to drive their trade, and would have come as long as coin was to be picked up.

I am not likely to forget that next morning, the 28th of August. It was a fine summer's morning, and there was just a little sea on, with a strongish breeze blowing from the eastward, but not enough to prevent boats coming off from Portsmouth. I counted forty sail-of-the-line, a dozen frigates and smaller ships of war, and well-nigh three hundred merchant vessels, riding, as of course we were, to the flood with our heads towards Cowes.

You will understand that under the lower deck was fitted a cistern, into which the sea-water was received and then pumped up by a hand pump, fixed in the middle of the gun-deck, for the purpose of washing the two lower gun-decks; the water was let into this cistern by a pipe which passed through the ship's side, and which was secured by a stop-cock, on the inside. It had been found the morning before that this water-cock, which was about three feet below the water line, was out of order and must be repaired.

The foreman came off from the dockyard, and said that it was necessary to careen the ship over to port sufficiently to raise the mouth of the pipe, which went through the ship's timbers below, clean out of the water, that he and his men might work at it. Between seven and eight o'clock the order was given to run the larboard guns out as far as they could go, the larboard ports being opened. The starboard guns were also run in amidships and secured by tackles, the moving over of this great weight of metal bringing the larboard lower-deck port-cills just level with the water. The men were then able to get at the mouth of the pipe. For an hour the ship remained in this position, while the carpenters were at work. We had been taking in rum and shot in the previous day, and now a sloop called the *Lark*, which belonged to three brothers, came alongside with the last cargo of rum; she having been secured to the larboard side, the hands were piped to clear lighter.

I had been on duty on the main-deck; several ladies had come off early in the morning, friends and relations of the officers. Some of them were either in the ward-room or gun-room, and others were walking the quarter-deck with the help of their gentlemen friends, as it was no easy matter, the ship heeling over as much as she was then doing. They thought it very good fun, how-ever, and were laughing and talking as they tried to keep their feet from slipping. I had been sent with a message to Mr. Hollingbury, our third lieutenant, who was officer of the watch; he seemed out of temper, and gave me a rough answer, as he generally did. He was not a favourite indeed with us, and we used to call him "Jib-and-Foresail Jack"; for when he had the watch at night he was always singing out, "Up jib," and "Down jib"; "Up foresail," "Down foresail"; and

from a habit he had of moving his fingers about when
walking the quarter-deck, we used to say that he had
been an organ-player in London. Just as I got back
to the main-deck, I caught a glimpse of a young lady
in black, leading a little boy; she turned her face
towards me, and I saw that she was the very same
who had come to my wife's cottage the previous
evening—indeed I should have known her by the little
boy by her side. I had to return to the quarter-deck
again, and when I once more came back to the main-
deck I could nowhere see her; but whether she went
into the ward-room, or had gone below, I could not
learn. I asked several people, for I thought she might
have brought me off a message from Susan, and I might
I fancied have been of use to her in finding the person
she wished to see. While I was looking about, Mr.
Webb, the purser's clerk, who had received orders to
go on shore in charge of a boat, came up and ordered
me to call the crew away; a couple of midshipmen
were going with him. This took up some time, and
prevented me from finding the young lady. Just then,
as I went up to report the boat gone to Mr. Hollingbury,
Mr. Williams, the carpenter, came up from the lower
deck, and requested that he would be pleased to order
the ship to be righted, as she was heeling over more

than she could bear. The lieutenant gave one of his usual short answers to the carpenter, who went below, looking as if he did not at all like it. He was back again, however, before I had left the deck, when he said in a short quick way, as if there was not a moment to lose—

"If you please, sir, the ship is getting past her bearings; it's my duty to tell you, she will no longer bear it."

"If you think, sir, you can manage the ship better than I can, you had better take the command," answered Mr. Hollingbury in an angry tone, twitching his fingers and turning away.

About this time there were a good many men in the waist who heard what the carpenter had said, and what answer the lieutenant gave. They all knew, as I did, that the ship must be in great danger, or the carpenter would not have spoken so sharply as he had.

A large number of the crew, however, were below; some on board the lighter, others at the yard-tackles and stay-falls, hoisting in casks; some in the spirit-room stowing away, others bearing the casks down the hatchway, all busy clearing the lighter. The greater number, it will be understood, were on the larboard side, and that brought the ship down still more to larboard. There was a little more sea on than before, which had begun to wash into the lower-deck ports, and, having no escape, there was soon a good weight of water on the lower deck. Several of the men, not dreaming of danger, were amusing themselves, laughing and shouting, catching mice, for there were a good many of them in the ship, which the water had driven out of their quarters. It's my belief, however, that the casks of rum hoisted in, and lying on the larboard side, before they could be lowered into the hold, helped very much to bring the ship down.

There stood the lieutenant, fuming at the way the carpenter had spoken to him. Suddenly, however, it seemed to occur to him that the carpenter was right, and he ordered the drummer to beat to quarters, that the guns might be run into their places, and the ship righted.

"Dick Tattoo" was shouted quick enough along the deck, for everyone now saw that not a moment was to be lost, as the ship had just then heeled over still more. The moment the drummer was called, all hands began tumbling down the hatchways to their quarters, that they might run in their guns.

Just then I saw a young midshipman, whom I had observed going off with Mr. Webb, standing at the

3

entrance-port singing out for the boat; he had forgotten
his dirk, he said, and had come back to fetch it.   The
boat, however, had got some distance off, and he was
left behind.   Poor fellow, it was a fatal piece of forget-
fulness for him.

"Never mind, Jemmy Fish," said little Crispo, one of
the smallest midshipmen I ever saw, for he was only
nine years old.   "There is another boat going ashore
directly, and you can go in her."

He gave an angry answer, and went back into the
gun-room, swearing at his ill-luck.

The men had just got hold of the gun-tackles, and
were about to bouse out their guns, which had been run
in amidship, some five hundred of them or more having
for the purpose gone over to the larboard side, which
caused the ship to heel still more, when the water made
a rush into the larboard lower-deck ports, and, do all
they could, the guns ran in again upon them.   Feeling
sure that the ship could not be righted, I, seizing little
Crispo, made a rush to starboard, and, dashing through
an open port, found myself outside the ship, which at
that moment went completely over, her masts and spars
sinking under the water.   Somehow or other, the young
midshipman broke from me and slipped over into the
sea.   I thought the poor little fellow would have been

lost, but he struck out bravely, which was, as it turned out, the best thing he could have done, as he could swim well.

I had just before seen all the port-holes crowded with seamen, trying to escape, and jamming one another so that they could scarcely move one way or the other. The ship now lying down completely on her larboard broadside, suddenly the heads of most of the men disappeared, they having dropped back into the ship, many of those who were holding on being hauled down by others below them. It was, you see, as if they had been trying to get out of a number of chimneys, with nothing for their feet to rest upon. Directly afterwards there came such a rush of wind through the ports that my hat was blown off. It was the air from the hold, which, having no other vent, escaped as the water pouring in took up its space. The whole side of the ship was, I said, covered with seamen and marines, and here and there a Jew maybe, and a good many women and a few children shrieking and crying out for mercy. Never have I heard such a fearful wailing. One poor woman near me shrieked out for her husband, but he was nowhere to be seen, and she thought that he was below with those who by this time were drowned; for there were hundreds who had been

on the lower decks, and in the hold, who had never
even reached the ports, and some who had fallen back
into the sea as it rushed in at the larboard side.   She
implored me to help her, and I said I would if I could.
We could see boats putting off from the ships all round
us to our help, and here and there people swimming
for their lives who had leaped from the stern-ports, or
had been on the lower deck.   I could not help thinking
of our fine old admiral, and wished that he might be
among them; but he was not, for he was writing in his
cabin at the time, and when the captain tried to let him
know that the ship was sinking, he found the door so
jammed by her heeling over that he could not open
it, and was obliged to rush aft and make his escape
through a stern-port to save his life.   This I afterwards heard.

As the ship had floated for some minutes, I began to
hope that she would continue in the same position, and
that I and others around me on her side might be saved.
I hoped this for my own sake, and still more for that
of my dear wife.   I had been thinking of her all the
time, for I knew that it would go well-nigh to break
her heart if I was taken from her, as it were, just before
her eyes.   Suddenly I found, to my horror, that the ship
was settling down; the shrieks of despair which rent

the air on every side, not only from women, but from many a man I had looked upon as a stout fellow, rang in my ears. Knowing that if I went down with the ship I should have a hard job to rise again, I seized the poor woman by the dress, and leaped off with her into the sea; but, to my horror, her dress tore, and before I could get hold of her again she was swept from me. I had struck out for some distance, when I felt myself, as it were, drawn back, and, on looking round, I saw the ship's upper works disappear beneath the water, which was covered with a mass of human beings, shrieking and lifting up their hands in despair. Presently they all disappeared. Just then I felt myself drawn down by someone getting hold of my foot under the water, but, managing to kick off my shoe, I quickly rose again and struck out away from the spot, impelled by instinct rather than anything else, for I had no time for thought; then directly afterwards up came the masts almost with a bound, as it were, and stood out of the water, with a slight list only to starboard, with the fore, main, and mizzentops all above water, as well as part of the bowsprit and ensign-staff, with the flag still hoisted to it. Many people were floating about, making for the tops and rigging, several of them terror-stricken, who could not swim, catching hold of those

that could.   I thought, on seeing this, that it would be
wiser to keep clear of them, till I could reach a boat
coming towards the wreck at no great distance off.   I
was pretty nigh exhausted when I reached the boat, in
which were a waterman and two young gentlemen, who
happened to be crossing from Ryde to Portsmouth at
the time.   They soon hauled me in, and I begged them
to pull on and save some of the drowning people.
As neither of them could row, quickly recovering I
took one of the oars, and was about to sit down to
help the waterman, when I saw, not far off, several
sheep, pigs, and fowls swimming in all directions,
while hencoops and all sorts of articles were floating
about.

"Let us save the poor beasts," cried one of the young
gentlemen thoughtlessly, just as young people are apt
to speak sometimes.   We, of course, took no heed of
what he said, when our fellow-creatures had to be
saved, and were pulling on when my eye fell on one of
the sheep swimming away from us, which seemed to
have someone holding on to its back.   We put the
boat round and followed, when, what was my surprise
to see a child hanging on with both its hands to the
sheep's back!   On a second look, it struck me that he
was the very same little boy I had seen at my cottage,

and who had come on board that morning with the
young lady.

"Gently, now," I cried out, afraid that the little
fellow might let go his hold before we were up to him,
but he held on bravely. In half a minute we were
alongside the sheep, and I had the child safely in my
arms. The young gentlemen hauled the poor sheep
into the boat, for it would not have done to let it drown
after having saved the child. I now saw that the
little fellow was the same I had supposed, for he had
his hat fastened on under his chin, and his sailor's
jacket and trousers on; he looked more astonished
than frightened, and when I asked him how he had got
into the water he could not tell me.

"Where is the young lady? is she your mother or
aunt?" I asked.

He had no answer to give, but only gazed about with
a startled look. He might have been younger than I
had supposed; at all events, not a word could I get out
of him to let me know who he was. One of the young
gentlemen wished to hold him in his arms, so I gave
the little fellow to him, and, taking the oar, we began
to pull back towards the wreck to try and save any
who might be still swimming about. The tops and
rigging were by this time full of people who had

managed to reach them, while several hanging on by
ropes were still floating in the water. A number of
boats from the men-of-war had, however, got up to the
spot, and they were better able to go in among the
spars and rigging than was our light wherry with the
sea which was then running. Now that I was safe
myself, I was anxious to learn who among my ship-
mates had escaped; but then I had the little boy to
look after, who was all wet and shivering, and I knew
too that the news of the accident would soon reach
Susan, and that she would be in a fearful state of alarm
if I did not let her know that I had been preserved.
I told the young gentlemen this, and begged them to
let the boatman put me and the child ashore at Ryde,
promising him a guinea if he would do so. They were
strangers who had been making a tour on the island,
and, though they were in a hurry to get back to
Portsmouth, they at once consented to do as I
wished.

As we had a fair wind we hoisted the sail, and, soon
getting away from the scene of the disaster, quickly
reached the hard at Ryde. After thanking the young
gentlemen and the waterman, I had jumped on shore
with the child in my arms, and was stooping down to
get hold of the sheep which I thought ought to be mine,

or rather the little boy's, when the waterman stopped me.

"No, no, master! you are not going to have that animal," he said ; "I want him."

"We should not have stopped to pick up the sheep if it had not been for the little boy," observed one of the young gentlemen ; "and so, as the sheep's life was saved on his account, the animal should go where he goes."

The waterman, however, seemed determined to have the sheep.

"Come, master," said I, "I will give you half a guinea, and that is as much as you will get for the animal."

The waterman still held out.

"Come, you shall have a guinea," said I, getting the money out of my pocket.

"And we will give five shillings apiece," said one of the young gentlemen.

"Come, that must settle the matter," said the other, giving the sheep a lift out of the boat.

Still the man grumbled, wanting to get more, but, handing the guinea to the young gentlemen, for the little boy being wet to the skin,—as of course I was, though that did not matter,—I wanted to be off home.

I got hold of the poor sheep and dragged it along, thinking thus to settle the matter. What had come over the waterman I do not know, but, springing out, he was going to catch hold of the sheep, when his foot slipped, and in he went between the boat and the hard.

"Go on, sailor, go on," cried the young gentlemen, laughing, while the waterman, now wet as I was, scrambled out, and, seeing that there was no use in following, got into his boat. Feeling very much obliged to the young gentlemen, and sorry I could not stop to thank them again, I hurried up as fast as I could to my home.

BEN CARRYING HARRY.

CHAPTER IV

A S I walked up the hill towards my cottage many people stopped, surprised at seeing me dripping wet, carrying a child and leading a sheep, and asked me all sorts of questions about the wreck; but I would not delay to answer them, except very briefly, or I should never have got home. I hoped that Susan would not have heard of the ship going down, still I half expected to meet her coming to learn if I had escaped; and I thought of the joy it would be to her to find that I was alive and well. As I drew near I saw that the cottage door was open; still Susan did not come out. My heart began to sink within me. I turned the sheep into the garden, and shut the wicket gate. I did not mind just then if the poor animal ate up all the flowers and vegetables; it deserved the best I could give it for the service it had rendered the little boy in my arms. No one was in the outer room, but I heard voices, and, opening the door of Susan's room, I saw Mrs. Leslie and

45

the two young ladies, with my sister Jane, standing by
Susan's bed.   Jane, catching sight of me, rushed out of
the room and threw her arms round my neck.

"Thank Heaven, you are alive, Ben!" she exclaimed.
"It will bring Susan to; don't be afraid.   The captain
has gone off for the doctor.   She saw the ship go down,
and went off in a faint, thinking that all on board must
be lost.   I, fortunately, was with her.   The captain, who
was looking through his glass at the time, also saw the
ship go over, and came down at once with the ladies to
comfort her, he intending to go off to Spithead to learn
all about the matter, and to hear if you had been
saved.   He, however, was first to go round to send
up the doctor, and that was the reason he missed
you."

"But, Ben," she asked, "is this the child Susan was
telling me about?   And the poor young lady, what has
become of her?"

I just told Jane what had happened; but I could not
say much, for all the time I was speaking I felt ready
to drop, thinking that maybe Susan was gone altogether, but that she had not the heart to tell me so.
I saw, however, that the ladies were burning feathers
and holding salts to her; and at last Mrs. Leslie came
out, and after I had told her all I had said to Jane,

with which she was much interested, she begged I would not be cast down, as she hoped my wife would soon again come round. She then went back to Susan's room, but soon returned.

"You may go in," she said, "and maybe, if she opens her eyes, the sight of you will do her more good than anything else."

I did as she bid me, but as I leaned over Susan my heart sank, for she did not seem to breathe at all, and looked so pale that I thought she must really be dead. Still the young ladies kept applying the burnt feathers and salts, and then one of them held a small looking-glass for a moment over her mouth, and showed me that there was breath on it, and that made me feel a little less miserable. At last the doctor came; he felt her pulse, and looked very grave; then he opened her mouth, and, having given her something, stood watching its effects.

Soon I could see that she was beginning to breathe, a slight colour having come back to her cheeks, and then she opened her eyes, but she seemed not to be looking at anything. Presently, however, she began to move them, and uttering a faint cry she sat up, and, throwing her arms around my neck, burst into tears.

"She will do now very well," said the doctor; and he

and the ladies left the room.   In a little time, however, they came back and called me out, telling Jane to go and sit with my wife.   The doctor showed me some physic bottles on the mantelpiece, and, saying that Jane knew what to do with them, he began to make inquiries about the wreck and the little boy, and how I had saved him.

I found that the ladies had got off his wet clothes, which Jane had hung up to dry before the fire, while they had wrapped him up in their shawls.   The only thing which the ladies found in his pockets was a little case.   On opening it they saw that it contained a picture—a likeness of the child himself, just as he was then dressed.   It was but slightly wet, as the water had not had time to soak it, so it was soon dried.

" It must be carefully preserved, as it may assist to prove who he is," observed Mrs. Leslie, though how that was to be was more than I could tell.   " It is slightly done in water-colours, evidently by a lady," observed Mrs. Leslie.

She examined it carefully, but could find no name either on the picture or the case.   It was placed on the mantelpiece to show to the captain as soon as he arrived.   Jane then took the child in to see Susan, who kissed him again and again, as if he were her own child restored to her, and from that moment she felt towards him almost as if she was his mother. Of course I had to go over the whole story again, but I could only narrate what I knew.

"We must wait to hear more till the captain comes back," said Mrs. Leslie. "He will be truly thankful to find that you have escaped, Ben, and then we will consider what must be done with this little child. Perhaps his father or mother may have escaped and will claim him, or the poor young lady who you say took him on board, though you think she was not his mother."

"Please, ma'm," I said, "though I cannot claim any merit for saving the child—for it was the sheep saved him—I would like that my wife should have charge of him, and I am sure she would, for she said so just now. I say it at once for fear anybody else should ask to have him and I suspect that there will be a good many who will make the offer."

"We will hear what the captain thinks," said Mrs. Leslie. "But you certainly have a better claim than anybody else, though, as I said before, probably some of his friends will come and claim him."

I thought so too, but I knew in the meantime that it would please Susan greatly to have charge of the little fellow.

4

At last the ladies, leaving Jane with us, returned home; and the doctor went to visit his other patients, saying he would look in again during the evening.

By that time Susan was able to sit up and tell me more about the young lady. She had got up very early in the morning, and, begging to have some breakfast for herself and the little boy, said that she wanted to pay a visit to a ship at Spithead, and would be back in the evening. She had gone away, taking her bag with her, but left a letter with a sovereign in it, and a few words to the effect that she wished to pay her rent and board in advance. This, Susan thought, she did that it might not be supposed that she was going away without paying.

I went down to the inn, at which we understood the young lady had left her trunk, but I could hear nothing of it; the landlord said that no such person as I described had come there. I made inquiries at other public-houses, thinking that there might be some mistake, but I got the same answer.

Late in the evening Captain Leslie came back, and, shaking me by the hand, told me that he had been afraid I was lost, and how glad he was I had escaped. He had been over to Portsmouth, and had visited the *Victory*, and other ships on board which the people

from the wreck had been carried, inquiring everywhere
for me. He had heard a great deal about the wreck
and the way in which many had been saved. I will
mention what he then told me, and what I picked up
from others.

Out of nearly a thousand souls who had been alive
and well on board the ship in the morning, between
seven and eight hundred were now lifeless. Besides
our gallant admiral, who had been drowned while
sitting writing in his cabin, three of the lieutenants,
including the one whose obstinacy had produced the
disaster, the larger number of the midshipmen, the
surgeon, master, and the major and several other
officers of marines, were drowned, as were some ladies
who had just before come on board. Sixty of the
marines had gone on shore in the morning, a consider-
able number of the rest who were on the upper deck
were saved, but the greater number of the crew, many
of whom were in the hold stowing away the rum casks,
had perished; indeed, out of the ship's whole complement,
only seventy seamen escaped with their lives.

I was sorry to hear that Mr. Williams, the carpenter,
whose advice, had it been followed, would have saved
the ship, was drowned; his body was picked up
directly afterwards, and carried on board the *Victory*,

where it was laid on the hearth before the galley-fire, in the hopes that he might recover, but life was extinct.

Captain Waghorn, though he could not swim, was saved. After trying to warn the admiral, he rushed across the deck and leaped into the sea, calling others to follow his example. A young gentleman, Mr. Pierce, was near him.

"Can you swim ?" he asked.

"No," was the answer.

"Then you must try, my lad," he said, and hurled him into the water.

Two men, fortunately good swimmers, followed. One of them getting hold of the captain, supported him, and swam away from the ship; the other fell upon Mr. Pierce, of whom he got hold and supported above water till the ship settled, when he placed him on the main-top, and both were saved. The captain, in the mean-time, was struggling in the water, and was with great difficulty kept afloat. A boat, with our seventh lieutenant, Mr. Philip Durham, had on the very instant the ship went over come alongside, when she was drawn down, and all in her were thrown into the water. Mr. Durham had just time to throw off his coat before the ship sank and left him floating among men and

hammocks. A drowning marine caught hold of his
waistcoat, and drew him several times under water.
Finding that he could not free himself, and that both
would be drowned, he threw his legs round a hammock,
and, unbuttoning his waistcoat with one hand, he
allowed it to be drawn off, and then swam for the main-
shrouds. When there he caught sight of the captain
struggling in the water, and a boat coming to take him
off he refused assistance, till Captain Waghorn and the
seaman supporting him were received on board. The
captain's son, poor lad, who had been below, lost his
life.

I heard that the body of the marine was washed on
shore ten days afterwards with the lieutenant's waistcoat round his arm, and a pencil-case, having his initials
on it, found safe in the pocket. There was only one
woman saved out of the three hundred on board, and
I believe she was the one I had helped out of the port;
her name was Horn, and I was glad to find that her
husband was saved also. It was curious that the
youngest midshipman, Mr. Crispo, and probably one
of the smallest children, our little chap, should have
been saved, while so many strong men were drowned.

I have known many a man come to grief through
having too much grog aboard; but one of the midship-

men, who had taken more than was good for him, having overslept himself at the Star and Garter on the beach at Portsmouth, when he awoke in the morning found that his ship was at the bottom, and most of his messmates drowned.

Our first lieutenant, Mr. Saunders, who had been busy in the wings, was drowned; his body, with his gold watch and some money in his pocket, was picked up, floating under the stern of an Indiaman off the Motherbank.

Of the three brothers who owned the sloop, two perished and one was saved. It was owing to her being lashed alongside that the ship righted, or she would have probably remained on her side. I was a good swimmer myself, and I should, had I not been, have lost my life long ago; and I have often thought what a pity it is that all seamen do not learn to swim. Many more might have been saved; but those who could not swim got hold of the men who could, and all were drowned together. If all had struck out from the ship when they found her going over, a greater number would have been picked up; instead of that, afraid to trust themselves in the water, they stuck by her, and they and a large number who got into the launch were drawn down with the ship, and all perished.

The foreman of the plumbers, whose boat was lashed head and stern, was with all his men drawn into the vortex as the ship went down, and not one of them escaped. It was a sad sight, ten days or a fortnight afterwards, to see the bodies which were picked up; some were buried in Kingston churchyard, near Portsmouth, and a large number in an open spot to the east of Ryde. Some time afterwards a monument was put up in Kingston churchyard, to the memory of the brave Admiral Kempenfelt and his ship's company. A court of inquiry was held, when Captain Waghorn was honourably acquitted, and it came out, that in so rotten a state was the side of the ship, that some large portion of her frame must have given way, and it is only a wonder that she did not go down before. When I come to think that she had upwards of one thousand tons of dead weight and spirits on board, it is surprising that she should have held together.

An attempt was made soon afterwards to raise the *Royal George,* and very nearly succeeded, as she was lifted up and moored some way from the spot where she went down; but a heavy gale coming on, some of the lighters sank, and the gear gave way, and she was again lost. It was whispered that on account of her rotten state the Admiralty had no wish to have her afloat, but that might have been scandal.

Having now said everything which people will care to hear about the fine old ship, I will go on with the history of the little boy saved from the wreck.

CHAPTER V

I MUST pass over the next seven years of my life and that of my young charge Harry, for that was the name Susan was certain the young lady called him. He sometimes spoke of himself as "Jack Tar," but probably he had heard his friends call him so, because he was dressed like a little sailor. We were puzzled what surname to give him. The captain and Mrs. Leslie and the young ladies and Susan and I talked it over, and at last settled to call him George, after the old ship; one of the young ladies thought St. for saint would sound better, and so he went by the name of "Harry St. George."

I was at first greatly afraid that he would be taken from us, for a subscription was made for the families of those who perished when the ship foundered, and when his story was known a good share was given to him, besides other contributions, and many people wanted to have him. The captain stood my friend, as

he did in all other matters, and insisted that as I pulled
him out of the water, and the only friend of his we
knew of had stopped at our house, Susan and I ought
to have charge of him. He would have taken him
himself, but he had a good many young children of his
own, and thought that Harry would do better with us,
and that he could still look after his education and
interests as he grew older.

As soon as Harry could speak, he said that he would
be a sailor, that his father was one, and that he would
be one too ; but who his father had been was a puzzle,
as about that, of course, he really knew nothing. He
could not tell us either anything about those he had
seen on board, or how he had got hold of the sheep,
though it is my belief that someone must have placed
him on the animal's back, intending to lash him to it,
but that the ship had gone down before there was time
to do so. Perhaps it was the last act of the poor young
lady, or maybe of his father, if his father, as seemed
probable, was on board.

As may be supposed, that sheep was a great pet with
us and the captain's family as long as it lived. Harry
was very fond of it, and would ride about on its back,
holding on just as he had done when the creature saved
him from drowning. People used to come and see him

ride about, and the ladies made a gay silk collar for the sheep, and also a bridle, but Harry would not use it, and always held on by the wool, saying that the sheep always well knew where to go. I railed off a piece of the garden and laid it down in grass, and on one side I built a house for the animal ; but as there was not food enough in the little plot, the captain had it up to a paddock near his house, where it used to scamper about with Harry on its back and enjoy itself.

"It's an ill wind that blows no one good," and people used to say that the foundering of the *Royal George* was a fortunate circumstance for the sheep, as it would long before have been under the butcher's knife.

The captain, meantime, made all the inquiries he could to try and discover the friends of the little fellow, but in vain ; none of those who were saved remembered to have seen the young lady talking to anyone, though two or three recollected seeing her, as I had, coming on board.

Susan, like a thoughtful woman as she was, would not let the little boy wear out his clothes, but at once set to work to make him a new suit, while she carefully laid up those he had had on, with his hat, and the little picture in the case, to assist, as she said, in proving who he was should any of his relatives appear. Still time

went on, and there appeared less chance of that than
ever.

I spent a very happy time on shore with Susan: as
we had no children of our own, we loved Harry as
much as if he was our own son. Still I could not be
idle; had it not been, indeed, for the captain, I should
have been pretty soon pressed and compelled to go to
sea, whether I liked it or not. Susan would have
gladly kept me at home, which was but natural; still,
I was too young to settle down in idleness, and should
have grown ashamed of myself; so, as seamen were
badly wanted for the navy, I at last entered, with
the captain's advice, on board a fifty-gun ship, the
Leander, he promising to use his influence to obtain a
boatswain's warrant for me. While I was serving on
board her we had a desperate action with a French
eighty-gun ship, the *Couronne*, when we lost thirteen
killed, and many more wounded, but succeeded in
beating her off and putting her to flight.

Peace came soon after this, and five years passed
before I obtained my warrant as boatswain. The prize-
money I had received enabled me in the meantime to
keep Susan and Harry as I wished; and when I
became boatswain she was able to draw a fair sum of
money every year. During those years I spent five

months at home, which was a pretty long time considering what generally falls to the lot of seamen.

Harry had grown into a fine manly boy, and the more I looked at him the more convinced I felt that he was of gentle birth; he called Susan mother, and me father, though he knew that we were not his parents. He had good manners, and, considering his age, a fair amount of learning, for he used to go up every day to the captain's to receive instruction from the children's governess. At last the captain considered that he ought to be sent to school, and arranged that he should go with his own son, Master Reginald, who was about his age, though Harry was the strongest, and, I may say, the most manly of the two.

While I was at home I taught Harry as much as he could learn of what I may call the first principles of seamanship,—to knot and splice, and box the compass. I also built and rigged a model ship, of which he was very fond.

"You will not forget all I have taught you, my boy," I said, when I was going off to sea.

"No, indeed I will not, father," he answered; "and when you come back I hope I shall have learnt more, for I will do my best to pick up information from everybody who will teach me. The captain, I know, will, when I come home for the holidays, and there is old Dick Wright, who has been at sea all his life, settled near us, and he will tell me anything I ask him; though there is no one teaches me so well as you do, father."

In those piping times of peace the ships were not kept so long in commission as they were during the war, so after serving three years as boatswain of the *Huzzar* frigate, on the West India and North American station, I once more returned home. I found Harry more determined than ever to go to sea, and he told me that Reginald Leslie had made up his mind to go also.

" Does his father wish it ? " I asked.

" Oh yes, he has no objection to his going; and do you know, father, the captain says that he will get him and me appointed to the same ship with you, provided she is sent to a healthy station," was the answer.

" Well, Harry, I shall be very glad to have charge of you both, and I am pleased that the captain thinks so well of you; though, to be sure, he has always shown that," said I.

Susan was much cast down at the thoughts of losing Harry, but she could not help acknowledging that it was time he should go to sea, if he was going at all.

" But a ship's boy has a hard life of it, as you have

often told me, Ben," she said, " and he has been gently nurtured, and brought up, I may say, like a young gentleman."

" And a young gentleman he will still remain; for, you may depend on it, the captain intends to get him placed on the quarter-deck; and, though he himself has retired from the service, he has interest enough to get me and the lads appointed to some ship commanded by a friend of his own; and I flatter myself that, from the certificate I got from my last captain, he will have no difficulty about that."

We had almost given up any expectations of ever meeting Harry's friends. I own that I did not care very much about this, for once on the quarter-deck I felt sure he would make his own way; and though it might be of advantage to him to find them out, it was possible that it might be very much to the contrary.

I was one day going up the street of Ryde with Harry, when we saw a crowd of women and children and a few men and boys standing round the model of a full-rigged ship, and we heard a loud voice singing out—

> " Cease, rude Boreas, stormy railer;
> List, ye landsmen all, to me;
> Messmates, hear a brother sailor
> Sing the dangers of the sea."

Then came the sound of a fiddle, and the singer continued his song to his own accompaniment.

"Let us stop and hear the old sailor," said Harry, drawing me towards the crowd.

We found room just opposite where the man was standing. I then saw that he had a timber leg, and that the ship was placed on a stand with a lump of lead fixed to the end of a bent iron rod at the bottom, which made it rock backwards and forwards.

"Oh yes! oh yes! all you good people, lend a ear to poor Jack's yarn," he continued; "and you pretty girls with the blue eyes and rosy cheeks, and you with the dark ones, who does more harm with your blinkers, when you've the mind, among the hearts of young fellows than ever our ships gets from the guns of the Frenchmen. There aren't many men in the navy of Old England who has seen queerer sights, or gone through more ups and downs in life than the timber-toed old tar who stands afore you, and who lost his leg in action aboard the *Thunderer*, seventy-four, when we took a Frenchman and hauled down his colours afore he knew where he was. There aren't many either, I've a notion, who've been worse rewarded, or more kicked about by cruel fate, or you wouldn't find him playing the fiddle and singing songs for your amusement.

BEN AND HARRY FIND JERRY WITH HIS MODEL SHIP AND FIDDLE.

Howsomdever, that's neither here nor there, and I daresay you wish to hear the end of his stave, and so you shall when each on you has helped to load this here craft with such coppers oɪ ᴗixpences or shillings as you may chance to have in your pockets, and I daresay now a golden guinea wouldn't sink her. Just look at her, always a-tossing up and down on the salt sea; that's what we poor sailors have to go through all our lives. She's a correct model of the *Royal George*, that famous ship I once served aboard when she carried the flag of the great Admiral Lord Hawke; and which now lies out there at Spithead fathoms deep below the briny ocean, with all her drownded crew of gallant fellows, no more to hear the tempest howling, or fight the battles of their king and country!"

I had been looking hard at the old sailor, whose eye just then falling on me, he recognised me at once as a brother salt.

"What, Jerry Dix!" I exclaimed; he looked at me very hard. "Don't you know me, old ship? have you forgotten little Ben Truscott?"

"What, Ben, my boy! Give us your flipper, old chum. I thought as how I had seen you afore when my blinkers first caught sight of you, but I didn't like to make a wrong landfall," he exclaimed.

We shook hands heartily. I was truly glad to see
the old man again.

"I see that you have become a warrant officer,"
he said, eyeing my uniform. "That's better nor
nothing, though I did think as how you'd have been
higher up the ratlines. And are you at anchor
hereabouts ? "

I told him that I was living in the neighbourhood,
and begged him to come at once to my cottage and
see my missus, and have a talk about old times.

"In course I will, Ben," he answered. Then
recollecting his audience, he thought that some
apology was necessary for leaving them so abruptly;
turning round, therefore, and eyeing his model of
the *Royal George*, as he called her, though she
was more like a frigate than a line-of-battle ship,
he said—

" You'll excuse me, ladies and gentlemen, but you
see as how I've fallen in with an old ship, who I've
known as man and boy these twenty years, so I must
just now keep him company; but I'll come back
to-morrow and finish that there stave I was a-singing,
and spin you more of my wonderful yarns, if you'll
just be good enough to come here and meet me; now
mind, my little dears, bring plenty of coppers; and

you, my pretty girls, bring something in your purses
for poor Jack; I never takes no money from ugly
ones—it's a rule of mine, it's wonderful too how few
I ever see's; so good-bye, and blessings on all of
you; and now, Ben, we'll up anchor and make sail."

Jerry on this unshipped his model from the stand,
which he took under his arm, while he placed the
vessel on his shoulder, and with a stout stick in his
hand came stumping on alongside me.

"Well, Jerry, I am truly glad to see you," I said;
"what have you been doing with yourself since we
parted?"

"That would be a hard matter to say, Ben, except
as how I've been knocking about the country from
east to west, and north to south, spinning yarns
without end, and singing and fiddling, and doing all
sorts of odd dodges to pick up a living. They were
honest ones though, so don't be afraid."

"And the yarns were all quite true, Jerry, eh?" I
could not help asking.

"As to that, maybe I have spun a tough one now
and then," answered Jerry, with a quizzical look.

"About losing your leg aboard the *Thunderer*, for
instance," I remarked.

"Well, I can't say quite so true as that, for I did

lose my leg aboard the *Thunderer*. To be sure, it was my wooden one. Why, don't you mind, Ben, how you got a mop-stick and helped me to splice it? It sounds better too, do you see, to talk of the *Thunderer*. The name tickles the people's ears, and it wouldn't do to tell 'em I lost my leg by falling down the main hatchway when half-seas over; so, do you see, I generally sticks to the *Thunderer* story, as it's nearer the truth than any other, and doesn't so much hurt my conscience."

I had till then forgotten the circumstance, and I felt that it would not do to press old Jerry too hard. I introduced him to Susan, who made him welcome, for she had often heard me speak about the old man; she soon got tea ready, and a few substantials; then I got out a bottle of rum and mixed some grog, which I knew would be more to his taste. He was very happy, and many a long yarn he spun. Harry listened to them eagerly, and seemed much taken with him. I must remark that, after Jerry had sat talking with us for some time, he completely changed his tone and style of speaking; and though he still used what may be called sailor's language, it was such as an officer or any other educated man might have employed. Indeed, I remembered that in my early days, Jerry, when in a serious mood, often showed that he was much superior in mind to the generality of people in the position in which he was placed. He afforded a melancholy example of the condition to which drunkenness and idle habits may reduce a man, who, from birth and education, might have played a respectable part in life.

"That's a fine boy of yours," observed Jerry when Harry had gone out of the room. "I don't set up for a prophet, but this much I'm sure of, that if you get him placed on the quarter-deck, he will be a post-captain one of these days. Is he your only one?"

I of course told Jerry that he was not my son, and described how he was rescued from the *Royal George.*

"Well, that's a surprising history," said Jerry; "it's a wonder I never heard of it. Do you see, I was at the time down in the West of England, where my family used to live; and I thought I would go and have a look at the old place and see if any of them were above-ground—not that I intended to make myself known. Few of my relatives would have wished to own a broken-down one-legged old tar like me. I found a brother a lawyer, and a cousin a parson, and two or three other relations; but, from what I heard,

I thought I should 'get more kicks than ha'pence' if I troubled them, so I determined to 'bout ship and stand off again. I was, howsomdever, very nearly being found out. I had got this here craft, which I called the *Conqueror* in those days, and was showing her off and spinning one of my yarns, when who should appear at the door of a handsome house but a lady with several little girls like fairies, and two fine boys. She and the young ones came down the steps, and after listening for some time she said in a pleasant voice, taking one of the youngsters by the hand—

"'This boy is going to sea some day, and we wish him to hear about sailors, and I know what you tell about them is true, for I once had a brother who went away to sea, and used to write to me and give me accounts of what happened. Poor fellow! he lost his leg just as you have done, and after that I heard no more from him, so that I fear he died.'

"'That was very likely, marm,' said I. 'In case I might have fallen in with him, may I be so bold to ask his name?'

"The lady, as I had a curious feeling she would, told me my own name, and then I knew for certain that she was my youngest sister Mary, the only one of the family who pitied me when others had cast me off. I had a hard matter not to make myself known, but I thought to myself that it would do no good to those pretty young ladies and gentlemen to find out their weather-beaten, rough old uncle. Mary herself, too, I had a notion would not have been really pleased; though, bless her gentle heart, I was sure that she would have been kind to me; and so I gulped down my feelings, and declared that I remembered a man of that name, who was dead and gone long ago. The words stuck in my throat, howsomdever, as I spoke them; and I was obliged to wish her good-morning and stump off, or she would have found me out. I hadn't got far before she called me back, and putting a five-shilling piece in my hand she said—

"'Pray accept this trifle, my good man, for the sake of my lost brother, for I know what you tell me is true, and that you are a genuine sailor.'

"'May Heaven bless you, my dear,' says I—I was as near as possible popping out the word 'Mary,' but I checked myself in time, and said 'lady' instead. The tears came to my eyes, and my voice was as husky as a bear's. She thought it was all from gratitude for her unexpected gift, and that I wasn't accustomed to receive so much. To be sure, she did look at me rather curiously, and, as I was going away,

on turning my head I saw that she was still standing
on the doorsteps watching me.

" I stopped about the neighbourhood for better than
a fortnight, for I could not tear myself away ; it was a
pleasure to get a sight of Mary driving about in her
carriage with her little girls, and her fine boys on
ponies trotting alongside. She was happily married,
I found, to a man of good fortune.

" While I was putting up at 'The Plough,' which I
had known well in my youth, I heard a number of
things about the neighbouring families, for I was
curious to learn what had become of all the people I
had known. There were not many of those who
frequented the house who could read, and there was no
newspapers taken in, and that is how I did not come
to hear about the *Royal George* till some time afterwards. It strikes me, though I may be wrong, that by
a wonderful chance I got hold of something which
has to do with this fine lad here, who you have
been looking after. I will think the matter over,
and try and rake up what I have heard ; but I don't
want to disappoint you, and I may be altogether
wrong."

I was naturally curious, and tried to get more out
of Jerry, but he would not say a word beyond repeating

over again that he might be altogether out of his reckoning. I of course begged him to stop with us, promising him board and lodging as long as he liked to stay; for, as he was in no ways particular, I could easily manage to put him up. He thanked me heartily, and said he would stop a night or two at all events. In the evening he went back with me to the inn to get his traps, for he travelled with a sort of knapsack, which he left behind him when he went out for his day's excursions.

The next morning he had a wash and shave, and turned out neat and trim, with a clean shirt and trousers, and altogether looked a different sort of person to what he had been the day before.

"You see, Ben, I have given up drinking, and like to keep a best suit of toggery, and to go to church on a Sunday in a decent fashion, which I used not to care about once upon a time. It's little respect that I can pay to the day, but I don't play my fiddle, nor sing songs, nor spin long yarns about things that never happened, as I think myself a more respectable sort of chap than I used to be."

I was glad to hear Jerry say this of himself, though maybe his notion that it was allowable to spin long yarns which had, as he confessed, no foundation in

truth, on other days in the week, was not a very correct
one. I told him so.

"As to that," he answered, "my hearers don't take
my yarns for gospel any more than the tales they read
in books. Some people write long yarns which aren't
true, and I spin much shorter ones out of my mouth.
Where's the difference, I should like to know? Mine
don't do any mortal being the slightest harm, and
that's more than can be said of some books I've fallen
in with. My yarns go in at one ear and out at the
other, and, supposing them worse than they are, they
can't be dwelt upon like those in books. I never speak
of a real man except to praise him; and if I paint a
scoundrel, I always give him a purser's name. I
produce many a hearty laugh, but never cause a blush
to rise on a maiden's cheeks; and so, Ben, don't be
hard on me."

I confessed that he had made out a good case, and
that I was wrong to find fault with him. At this he
seemed much pleased, and, laughing heartily, told me
that I reminded him of the little boy who wanted to
teach his grandfather to suck eggs.

Jerry had been so accustomed to wandering about,
that though Susan did her best to make him comfort-
able, and he always found a willing listener in Harry,

after he had been with us three days he began to weary
of staying quiet, and announced that he must get under
way. The next morning he appeared in his weekday
clothes, shouldering his knapsack and model ship.
After wishing us all good-bye, he trudged off, intending,
as he said, to go to the west end of the island.

"You will not forget that matter about Harry?"
I said.

"No fear, Ben! It's the main thing I have on my
mind; and if I succeed in picking up any information,
I will let you know—depend on that," he answered.
"Heaven bless you, and Susan and the boy!"

We watched him as he trudged sturdily away over
the hills towards the town, having, I observed, again
assumed his independent, happy-go-lucky air, which
he had laid aside during his stay with us.

CHAPTER VI

HARRY had been greatly taken with Jerry, and seemed to miss him very much. He used to go out most days to play with his schoolfellow, the captain's son; but while Jerry was with us he preferred stopping and listening to his yarns. The time, however, for both the boys to return to school was now approaching. I saw that Harry had something on his mind.

"Father," he said, "am I not old enough to go to sea? and, if I am, had I not better be looking out for a ship?"

"As we are no longer fighting the French, there are not many put in commission," I observed; "so maybe you will have to wait for some time."

As it happened, the very next day I got an order to join the *Nymph*, thirty-six gun frigate, just commenced fitting out at Portsmouth, commanded by Captain Edward Pellew.

"So soon, Ben!" said Susan, looking pale as soon as she saw the letter; "I thought you would have had a longer spell on shore; but I am thankful it's peace time, and I shall not be trembling at the thoughts of your having to fight the French."

"That's the very thing we would rather be doing, my dear girl," I answered, smiling, and trying to raise her spirits.

I at once went up to the captain and told him.

"I am glad of it," he answered. "There is not a better officer in the service than Captain Pellew, and, as he is a friend of mine, I have no doubt that I shall be able to get him to take the two youngsters. I will go over to Portsmouth this very day and see about it."

As I had to join at once, the captain took me over in his wherry. In about a couple of hours he came on board, and told me it was all settled, and he should trust to me to look after his son as well as Harry, as he was sure I should do my best for the lad.

I had taken lodgings for Susan, and she joined me two days afterwards, bringing Harry with her. She had plenty to do in preparing his outfit, and that kept her mind from dwelling too much on our approaching parting. Harry was the first midshipman to join, and he had the advantage of seeing the ship fitted out from the beginning. The captain brought Reginald over about a week later, and Harry was proud in being able to teach him all he knew. He had thus as it were got the lead, and he kept it, though he did not let Reginald feel that he thought himself superior to him in any way. The two lads were fast friends, as they had always been, for both were honest, kind-hearted, and good-tempered. There was no difficulty in getting hands; and as I knew where to find the best men, we soon had a first-rate ship's company without much pressing.

We stood down Channel, bound out for Lisbon, with some official characters on board. The captain's great aim was to get the ship's company into good order, and we were continually exercising the guns and shortening and making sail. This was an advantage to the youngsters, as they learnt much faster than they would otherwise have done. They used to come to my cabin, and I taught them all I could, though with my duties I had not much time to myself. I had advised Harry not to call me "father"; not that he should have been ashamed of his father being a boatswain had I been his father, but, as I was not, I thought it would be better for him to be independent. I felt for him the same as if he was my son. He and young Leslie got on very well in the berth, and, young as they were, gained the respect of their messmates. Thus a year or more passed by; we had visited Cadiz, and had taken a trip up the Mediterranean, when we were ordered home with despatches. One day I observed Harry was looking less merry than usual; I asked him what was the matter. At first he did not like to tell me. At last he said—

"The truth is, father, that my messmates have found out that I was saved when the *Royal George* went down, and that St. George is not my real name."

"Never mind that, Harry," I answered; "you have as much right to it as they have to theirs. Tell them you hope to make it some day as well known to fame as Hawke's, Collier's, or Rodney's."

Harry promised to follow my advice; at the same time he confessed that it made him more anxious than ever to find out who his parents really were, and whether or not they were both on board the *Royal George* when she went down.

"You tell me that you think the poor lady who took me on board was not my mother, and so perhaps my mother was on shore."

"But the young lady was in black, and so it's possible that your mother may have died, and that she

6

took you to see your father, to whom, for some reason or other, she wanted to introduce you. That's how I read the riddle, but maybe I am mistaken."

Harry was satisfied.

"When we return to England, you will try and get Jerry Dix to come to see you, and learn if he has heard anything more?" he said.

Of course I replied that I would if I could; but that Jerry Dix had not left me any address, and it might be a hard matter to find him. I did not think that he had played me false, but I was afraid that some accident might have happened to him, or that he might be dead, and then the clue which he fancied he had found would be lost.

After visiting Cadiz and Gibraltar, we were on our way home, just entering the chops of the Channel, after being kept at sea by calms and contrary winds for three weeks or more, when a frigate hove in sight and hoisted English colours. She made her number, and we knew her to be the thirty-two gun frigate *Venus*. Captain Faulknor, who commanded her, came on board, and we soon heard the news. The French Republicans had risen up against their king, and cut his head off, and as the English Government did not approve of that, they had ordered the French ambassador to leave

the country. The National Convention, as it was
called, had therefore declared war against Great
Britain, and we were now going to thrash the French
Republicans soundly, wherever we could find them,
afloat or on shore.

This was, of course, considered to be glorious news;
and all hands fore and aft were in high glee at the
thoughts of the work cut out for us.

The *Venus* soon after parted company with us to go
and look out for the enemy, while we made the best of
our way up Channel to Portsmouth, to fill up with
ammunition and stores. Before Susan could come
over to see me we had sailed for the westward. On
our way down Channel we again fell in with the *Venus*,
which had had a sharp action with two French frigates,
the *Sémillante* and *Cléopâtre*, when she beat off the
first, and escaped from the latter. We sailed together
in search of the two frigates. We sighted them three
days afterwards, when they, having nimble heels,
escaped us and got into Cherbourg.

Having cruised together for some time, we parted
company, and we put into Falmouth. We had now
been a year in commission, and all hands were eager
to meet an enemy of equal force. My fear was for
Harry; I don't know how I should have felt had he

been my own son, but I doubt that I should have been as anxious as I was about him, and I knew it would go well-nigh to break Susan's heart should he be killed.

He and Reginald were in high spirits, and could talk of nothing else but the battle in which they hoped to be engaged, and were always asking me questions about those I had seen fought in my younger days. You see, after the long peace, we had a good many officers and men on board, who had never seen a shot fired in anger.

Our captain, however, and his brother, Commander Israel Pellew, had been through the American War of Independence while they were midshipmen; the latter had lately joined us as a volunteer. We sailed again on the 17th of June on a cruise. When nearly abreast of the Start we stood out for the southward, in the hopes of falling in with one of the two frigates we had chased into Cherbourg. We were about six leagues from the Start, when the lookout from the masthead hailed—

"A sail on the starboard beam."

This was as we were standing to the south-east. You may be sure that we at once bore up in chase, under all sail. The stranger, as we got nearer, was seen carrying a press of canvas, as we fancied, to get away from us. We came up with her, however, and by the evening made her out to be no other than the *Cléopâtre*, one of the frigates of which we were in search. Finding that she could not escape, even if she intended to do so, she hauled up her foresail, and lowered her topgallant - sail, bravely waiting for us. The men were at quarters, and the officers at their stations, while the captain conning the ship stood at the gangway with his hat in his hand. We were close up to each other and not a shot had been fired; the French captain hailed, when our captain cried out—

"Ahoy! ahoy!"

On which our crew gave three hearty cheers, and shouted—

"Long live King George!"

"Reserve your fire, my lads, till you see me put my hat on my head," cried our captain; "then blaze away and thrash the Frenchmen as soon as you can."

The word was passed along the deck, and all hands eagerly looked out for the signal.

The Frenchmen tried to imitate our cheer, but made a bad hand of it. Captain Mullon, as we afterwards heard was his name, the commander of the French frigate, was seen holding the red cap of liberty in his hand, and making a speech to his crew, on which

they all sang out at the top of their voices, *Vive la
République,* and one of the sailors, running up the main
rigging, secured the red cap to the masthead. We
stood on till our foremost guns could bear on the
starboard quarter of the enemy.

The French captain held his hat, like our captain, in
his hand. They bowed to each other, when ours was
seen to place his on his head. It was the looked-for
signal. At that instant we opened fire, which the
Frenchmen were not slow in returning. We were
running before the wind, within rather less than hailing
distance of the Frenchman, who was on our larboard
beam. In little more than half an hour we had shot
away the Frenchman's mizzenmast and wheel; but our
mainmast was badly wounded, and every instant I
expected it to fall. Having lost command of her rudder,
the *Cléopâtre* fell aboard us, her jib-boom passing through
our fore and mainmast. I thought that this would
finish our mainmast, but, fortunately, the Frenchman's
jib-boom gave way.

We were blazing away all this time, raking the
Cléopâtre fore and aft. We had lost a good many
officers and men, and I saw two midshipmen knocked
over not far from me. I looked out for Harry and
Reginald Leslie, and I caught sight of them, still stand-

ing unharmed amid the smoke, but I had not much time even to think about them or anything else except my duty.

We now fell alongside the enemy head and stern, being still foul of each other. Her larboard-maintop-sail studden-sail-boom iron having hooked the leach-rope of our maintop-sail, I had still good reasons to tremble for our mainmast. I saw a youngster spring aloft. It was Harry. He made his way along the yard, and with his knife cut the leach-rope; and though many a shot from the Frenchmen was fired at him, he came down safely. I felt my heart beat with pride as I saw him, for he had saved the mast. The next moment the cry was heard—

"Boarders, away!"

Our brave first lieutenant, Mr. Norris, leading the boarders, cutlass in hand, leapt from the quarter-deck on to the forecastle of the French frigate, while our master, Mr. Ball, at the head of another party, made his way through the bow-ports of the enemy. On they rushed, one party on the upper and the other on the main-deck, sweeping all before them. The Frenchmen, though they numbered half as many again as our crew, gave way; some springing down the hatchway, others flying aft, and in fifty minutes from the commencement of the action the Republican colours were hauled down, and the Frenchmen from all directions cried for quarter.

The brave French captain was found lying on the deck, his back torn open by a round shot, and part of his hip carried away. He was seen gnawing at a piece of paper, which he continued to bite till his hand dropped, and, his head sinking down, he ceased to breathe. He fancied that he was destroying a list of coast signals used by the French, which he had found in one of his pockets; but he was mistaken, for the paper he wished to prevent falling into our hands was discovered on him covered with blood. He was a brave fellow—there was no doubt about that. We had not gained our victory without a heavy loss, for we had eighteen seamen and marines, three midshipmen and two other officers, killed, and twenty-seven wounded; while the French lost sixty-three men. I do not think there was ever during the war a more equal or better-fought battle, except that the Frenchmen had eighty more men to begin with than we had; but then the *Nymph* had slightly heavier metal, and was a few tons larger than our antagonist. However, I believe that if it had been the other way, we should, notwithstanding, have won the day.

As soon as we had repaired damages we made sail, though it was four days before we reached Portsmouth with our prize. The brave French captain was buried the next day in Portsmouth churchyard, the surviving officers being permitted to attend him to the grave. A few days afterwards His Majesty, George the Third, came aboard our frigate, when our captain and his brother, Commander Pellew, and all the officers of the ship, were presented to him.

The king was highly pleased with the way the action had been fought, and at once knighted our brave captain, and presented his brother with his commission as post-captain, while Lieutenant Norris was made a commander. The king made inquiries as to what others had done.

"They all did their duty, your Majesty," answered the captain.

"No doubt about it. That is what I know my officers and seamen always do," observed the king.

The captain then told him of the way Harry had behaved.

"I am pleased to hear it, my lad," said the king; "and I hope some day that I shall have the pleasure of placing the flat of my sword on your shoulders. What's your name?" asked the king.

The captain told him, and mentioned how he had been saved from the *Royal George*.

"What! are you the 'Child of the Wreck' I have been told of?" asked the king.   "I wish that more like you had been saved; you have begun well, and will prove an honour to the service, no doubt about that."

The king spoke in a like fashion to several others. As may be supposed, I felt prouder than ever of Harry, and was sure that if his life was preserved he would not disappoint the good king or anyone else.

CHAPTER VII

THE grass did not grow in the streets of Portsmouth in those busy times; I managed, however, to get leave to run over to Ryde for a couple of days, and took Harry and Reginald Leslie with me. The youngsters got a hearty welcome; and when I told the captain how Harry had behaved, he complimented him greatly. The youngsters were made much of by the ladies, and they ran no small risk of being spoilt, so it seemed to me. Miss Fanny especially, the captain's youngest daughter, seemed never tired of talking to Harry, and asking him questions which he was well pleased to answer. She was a pretty, fair-haired, blue-eyed little girl, about three years younger than him. Neither the captain nor his lady troubled themselves about the matter, looking upon them as children; of course they were not much more. Harry, however, came home in the evening to Susan and me, and I was pleased to see that he was not a bit set up, but just as affectionate to my wife as he had ever been.

The day after I got home I received the long-looked-for letter from Jerry; but there was not much in it which I could make out, except that he had come to an anchor near his old home, and had half-resolved not to go wandering any more.   He had made himself known to his sister, who was trying to persuade him to remain quiet.   He was very mysterious about the affair I had at heart.   He still insisted that he was on the right track; but as he might spoil all if it was discovered what he was about until the right time came, it would be wiser not to mention names, in case anybody should get hold of his letter.

"The youngster has friends," he added, "and is doing very well, and can wait without damage for a few years.   There is another person also for whose sake, even more than for his, I should like to have the mystery cleared up, but the risk is too great to make the attempt.   We must, therefore, as I have said, let both wait till the proper opportunity, and that is in the hands of One who orders all things for the best."

I should say that Jerry wrote in a very different way to that in which he spoke, and it seemed to me that when he got a pen in his hand he was no longer the rough sailor, but the educated man he had once been before he got into bad ways and ran off to sea.

He signed his letter "J. D.," and told me to send my answer to the post-office, but on no account to direct my letter by the name I knew him by. I of course did as he desired, thanking him heartily for what he had already done, and expressing a hope that he would not neglect the interests of one whom my wife and I loved so much.

I have not time to describe one-tenth part of the events in young Harry's career.

After serving in the *Nymph* some time longer, I was transferred to the *Juno* frigate; and Captain Leslie succeeded in getting the two youngsters appointed to her. I had belonged to her when she was first in commission in the West Indies, commanded by Captain Hood. A braver man never stepped. I remember an incident which will show his character. We were lying at St. Anne's Harbour, Jamaica, a heavy gale of wind blowing, when the lookout from the masthead discovered far out at sea a raft tossing about on the foaming waves, which threatened every moment to wash off three men who were seen clinging to it. The captain at once ordered a boat to put off to their assistance, but the sea was so heavy that the boat's crew held back, thinking that they should lose their own lives if they made the attempt.

"I never order men to undertake what I dare not do myself," exclaimed Captain Hood, springing into the boat.

Away he pulled amid the foam-crested, tumbling seas. Every moment we thought that the boat and all on board would be lost; but he at last succeeded in reaching the raft, and taking the three poor men off it just as they were exhausted, and would have in another minute been washed away.

Such a man I was heartily glad to serve under again. We sailed immediately for the Mediterranean, where we joined Lord Hood's fleet lying in the harbour of Toulon. The French Royalists had given up the city to the English and Spaniards, who were at that time our allies, and their troops assisted to man the fortifications. A Republican army, however, invested the place, and a good deal of fighting had been going on. The English had, however, not quite two thousand men on shore, and, though they could trust the French Royalists, the Spaniards, Neapolitans, and other troops could not be relied on. Serving in the Republican army was Napoleon Buonaparte, then an officer of artillery; not that I knew of it at the time, but I afterwards heard that he had been there when he became Emperor of the French.

The French had one night surprised a detachment of Spanish troops posted on an important height above Toulon, and thereby got possession of it. No time was to be lost in driving them out, and the marines and a party of blue-jackets from the ships close at hand were ordered on shore to assist the Spaniards in storming the heights and turning out the Republicans. The seamen, twenty of whom went from our ship, were headed by Lieutenant Seagrave : I went to assist in the landing. We had shoved off, when I found that Reginald Leslie and Harry had jumped into the boat. Reginald said that he was resolved to see the fun. Harry told me that he had been ordered to take charge of the men instead of a master's mate, who was unable to go, so he was all right; but Reginald had no business to be where he was, and had there been time I should have sent him on board again. It was dark by the time we had reached the shore; the troops and blue-jackets, mustering eight hundred, formed as they landed, and were immediately ordered to push forward. I had intended, as in duty bound, to keep Reginald Leslie in the boat, but he leapt on shore among the first, and I was too busy to see what became of him. The hills which rose above our heads were steep and rugged, notwithstanding which, soldiers and blue-jackets pushed up them by a long and narrow path, with a rugged precipice on one side. At any moment they might arouse the enemy, who would soon have stopped their progress.

I knew it would take a couple of hours or more, from the distance they had to go, before the party could be back. I waited anxiously, thinking more perhaps of Harry and his messmate than of the success of the expedition, about which I had little doubt. The time seemed very long. At last, hearing the sound of firing from among the hills, I knew that the batteries were being attacked. The firing then ceased, the sound of only an occasional shot reaching my ears. I now waited more anxiously than before for the return of the party. Suddenly the sound of great guns and musketry came down from over the hills, and I began to fear that our party were being again attacked by a superior force. I had posted a couple of lookouts on the neighbouring heights which commanded the path, to give notice of the approach of either friends or foes. One of them came running down, crying out—

" They are coming, sir, they are coming ! "

" Our people or the French ? " I asked.

" Sure it must be our people, sir," answered the man, who was Irish but as he seemed somewhat doubtful about the matter, I ordered the men into the boats, to be ready to shove off, should by any chance our party have been cut off. At last I saw a large body of men coming down the hill, and was greatly relieved when I discovered that they were Spaniards, and that our other allies were following close behind. Soon afterwards the English troops came in sight, the bluejackets bringing up the rear. They were at once embarked, and I heard that they had stormed and captured the batteries, and spiked the guns, but had been attacked on their way back by a large body of Republicans, who, however, had been defeated with great loss. I anxiously looked out for the two midshipmen, but could nowhere find them. I made inquiries, and was told that they had been seen with the sailors, unhurt, just before the last attack, but that several men had fallen just as they had received orders to charge the enemy. It was very evident, I feared, that they had either been killed or taken prisoners. Still, as I could not bear the thoughts of leaving them, I obtained permission from the commanding officer to take a party of men and to go in search of them, as, should they have been only wounded, they might not be far off. I had plenty of volunteers, but chose only ten men, with a French Royalist officer who had been aboard our ship and

7

knew the country. There was no time to be lost, so we started at once up the steep path. I felt my heart greatly cast down, for I would have sooner lost my life than have had the brave boys cut off. Still I had some faint hopes of finding them; but should they have been taken prisoners by the Republicans, I had too much reason to fear that they would be shot; for those fellows were terrible savages, and many of their Royalist countrymen who had fallen into their hands had been mercilessly put to death. As we approached the spot where the Republicans had attacked our friends, we carefully examined the ground on either side. Pushing on, we came upon several dead bodies of men who had been shot, two or three of whom were Spaniards, the others Neapolitans ; and farther on were a still greater number of Republicans who had been killed in the attack on the troops ; still we went on till we got near the batteries, when our guide, though a brave man, refused to go farther, saying that we should probably lose our own lives, as the enemy were likely to be in the neighbourhood, and that it was most probable the midshipmen had been taken prisoners. Very unwillingly, therefore, I agreed to return. We still examined every place on either side of the road into which a person could have crept for concealment,

for my idea was that one of the youngsters had been
wounded, and that the other had refused to desert him.
All this time we had been careful not to speak above a
whisper, for fear, should an enemy be in the neighbourhood, of giving notice of our approach. We had got
more than half-way down the hill, when, just as we
turned a sharp angle of the path, I caught sight,
through the gloom, of a figure, some fifty yards ahead of
us, moving on, it seemed slowly; the person, whoever
he was, must have heard our footsteps, for he appeared
to run on, we of course making chase; presently he
stopped, and the next instant we lost sight of him.
Some of the men fancied that he must have gone over
the precipice. We were quickly up to the spot, and
were speaking pretty loudly about what had become of
the man, when I heard a voice crying out my name,
and, turning round, there in a hole of the rock I
discovered Harry supporting Reginald in his arms.

"Thank Heaven!" he exclaimed; "I thought you
were Republicans, and that we should have been taken
off by them."

All hands were very glad to find the young gentlemen, but we lost no time in talking. It had been just
as I had supposed; Reginald had been wounded, and
falling by the edge of a bank had rolled down it, and

Harry, who had been at his side at the time, followed him. Just then the Republicans who had been coming up had charged our men, and, in the darkness, the lads being unable to tell which party had gained the victory, they had been afraid to climb up the bank till all was again silent. By this time Reginald's wound prevented him from walking, and Harry had had great difficulty in getting him up the bank; he then had taken him on his shoulders, intending to carry him down the hill, but when he had got some way Reginald fainted from pain and loss of blood. On this he had carried him to a copse on the hillside, some little way off; here he had put him down, and had done his best to bind up his wound, intending to go on again as soon as Reginald was somewhat recovered. He had heard us hunting about, but thinking that we might be enemies he had kept silent, though it was a wonder that no one had discovered the youngsters. After we had passed by, Reginald having come to, Harry had taken him on his back, and was proceeding down the hill when he overtook them as I have mentioned. We, of course, lifted up Reginald, and hurried as fast as we could down to the boat.

Harry, as he deserved, gained great credit for the

way he had behaved, for he had undoubtedly saved
Reginald's life; and, in consideration of his wound, the
captain forgave Reginald for having left the ship
without leave.

I never had a fancy for fighting on shore, and I was
not sorry when we were ordered to Malta, to bring
away a party of Maltese marines, engaged to serve on
board the fleet.

We had light and unfavourable winds going, and, on
returning with the soldiers aboard, we met with a
succession of strong contrary gales from the eastward,
and a lee current, which prevented us from arriving
abreast of the harbour's mouth till about ten o'clock at
night on the 11th of January. The captain, not wishing
to run the risk of being thrown to leeward, considering
the number of men we had on board, determined to
sail into the harbour at once. We had no pilot, but
the master felt confident that he could take the ship
in without risk. The hands were at their stations, and
the captain ordered Harry and another midshipman to
go forward with night-glasses and look out for the
fleet. We had a moderate leading wind, which sent
us under our topsails at a fair rate through the water.
As we neared the outer roads of Toulon we were
somewhat surprised at not seeing any of the fleet, but

the captain concluded that the ships had run for shelter into the inner harbour.

The night was clear, the moon was shining brightly, and the water smooth.   As we advanced we made out a brig ahead, and beyond her the lights of several others.   The captain, therefore, had no doubt but that he was right in his conjectures.   Having passed the forts, we were standing on, when we found that we could not weather the brig-of-war we had seen ahead of us.   We were close to her stern, when a hail came from her, but what was said we could not make out. The captain, however, supposing that the brig was Spanish, and wanted to know what ship ours was, answered—

" His Britannic Majesty's frigate *Juno*."

Again a hail came from the brig, and several people shouted out, " Viva ! "   The captain then inquired what English ships were in the harbour, but we could not make out a word of what was said in reply ; still, of course, taking her for Spanish, this did not surprise us, except that it seemed somewhat strange that an English vessel should not have been stationed at the mouth of the harbour.   Just as we passed under the stern of the brig, someone again hailed from her—

" Luff ! luff ! "

The captain, fearing that we had shoal water aboard, ordered the helm to be put a-lee, but before the frigate got her head to the wind we were aground. The captain immediately ordered the sails to be clewed up and handed. While the people were on the yards, we caught sight of a boat pulling from the brig towards the town. Just then, before the people were off the yards, a sudden flaw of wind drove the ship's head off the bank. Hoping now to get off, the order was given to hoist the driver and mizzen-staysail, and to keep the sheets to windward. The instant the ship lost her way, the bower-anchor was let go, on which she tended to the wind; but the after-part of her keel was still aground. The launch and cutter were now hoisted out, and I jumped into the first to carry out the kedge-anchor, with two hawsers, in order to warp the ship clear. We worked away with a will, for we did not like the thoughts of being seen on shore by the rest of the fleet at daybreak. That was all we just then thought about. At length we succeeded in getting her completely afloat, and were returning to the ship, when we saw a boat go alongside, and being hailed, she answered, " Captain Someone," but we did not catch the name, and up the side he went with two other persons, who seemed to be officers. On reaching the deck he introduced himself as a French captain, and said that it was the regulation of the port, and according to the commands of the admiral, that vessels should go into another part of the harbour and do ten days' quarantine.

On this, Captain Hood asked where the *Victory*, the admiral's ship, lay. The French officer hesitated, and then said she was far up the harbour.

Just then Harry, who had a sharp eye, exclaimed somewhat loudly to a messmate—

"Why, the fellows have the Republican cockades in their hats!"

The captain overheard him; and, looking more earnestly at the Frenchmen's hats, he saw by the light of the moon,. to his dismay, the three Republican colours. He put another question about the admiral, when the French officer, finding that he and his companions were suspected, replied—

"Make yourselves easy; the English are good people, and we will treat them kindly; the English admiral has departed some time."

I can just fancy how our brave captain felt.

"We are prisoners!" exclaimed one of the officers; and the word, like wildfire, ran along the deck, while several of the officers hurried up to the captain to

learn the truth. We all knew what we had to expect—
a French prison till the end of the war, even if we
escaped being shot by the Republicans. I never felt
more cast down in all my life, and I believe that was
the case with everyone on board. To be caught like a
rat in a trap, without a chance of escape, seemed too
bad. We were all standing, not knowing what to do,
some proposing one thing and some another, expecting
the French boats to come alongside and take possession
of our tidy little frigate, when a flaw of wind came
down the harbour. Scarcely had we felt it than our
third lieutenant, Mr. Webley, exclaimed—

"I believe, sir, we shall be able to fetch out if we
can get her under sail."

"We will try it at all events, and Heaven grant we
may," answered the captain; "we will not give up
our ship without doing our best to save her. All
hands to their stations! Send the Frenchmen below."

I never saw such a wonderful change as in a moment
came over everybody on board. The Frenchmen began
to bluster and drew their sabres, but our jollies quickly
made them sheath them again, and they had to submit
with remarkably bad grace, hoping, I daresay, that we
should again get on shore. Officers and men flew to
their stations, and in less than three minutes we had

the canvas on her, and the yards braced ready for casting. The head sails filled.

"Cut the cable!" shouted the captain.

The ship quickly gathering way, began to glide down the harbour. Our launch and cutter, and the Frenchmen's boat, were at once cut adrift, so as not to impede us, while a favourable flaw of wind gave the ship additional way. We had still, however, the heavy batteries to pass, and it was not likely that they would allow us to go by without a warm peppering; not that we thought much about that, for I know my heart bounded as light as a cork, and so I am pretty sure did the hearts of everyone on board at the thoughts that we were free.

Directly we began to loose our sails, the French brig opened her fire, and we saw lights bursting out on all the batteries; while one, a little on the starboard bow, was blazing away at us. As we glided on, the guns of all the forts opened fire as they could be brought to bear. The wind was very scant, and it seemed impossible that we could weather the point without tacking, and, of course, while we were in stays, the enemy would have taken steady aim; but again a favourable flaw of wind helped us. As soon as the ship was well under command, the order was given to man the guns, and we began returning the enemy's fire with good effect, as far as we could judge. The Frenchmen's shot came flying through our sails, considerably cutting up our rigging, and two thirty-six pound shot struck our hull; but we repaired damages as fast as we could, and, nothing daunted, stood on. Wonderful to relate, all the time not a man had been hit; and if we felt happy when we first got the frigate under way, we had reason to be doubly so when we found ourselves clear of the harbour and not a ship following us. We should have had no objection to it had a frigate of our own size come out, as to a certainty we should have given her a sound drubbing, and finished by carrying her off as a prize.

CHAPTER VIII

I SHOULD spin far too long a yarn were I to describe the various actions in which we were engaged, or even mention the different ships to which we belonged. Both Harry and Reginald Leslie had now passed for lieutenants—indeed they had been for some time doing duty as such. Of course they could have done very well without me, but hitherto, thanks to Captain Leslie, we had always been appointed to the same ship.

The last time we were at home, Harry had become a greater favourite than ever with the captain's family. Of course the brave way in which he had saved Reginald at Toulon, at the risk of his own life, was well known. Though he himself might not have talked much about it, Reginald had given a full account of all that had happened. With Susan and me, Harry was just the same as he had always been. One thing we discovered, that he had given his heart to Miss Fanny, and it was Susan's belief that she had given hers in return. We saw no harm in this, though we thought it better not to talk to him about it; but I had a notion that the captain did not suspect the true state of the case. Both Harry and I were anxious to hear from Jerry, but day after day passed by, and no letter came from him; I was expecting to be sent off to sea, and so were the young gentlemen. Harry, I suspect, was in no hurry to go; and Reginald, who generally took things easy, was happy with his family, and was thankful to stop on shore for a spell. Still the accounts which we read in the papers, of the gallant actions fought, made us before long wish to be afloat again. We were reading, I remember, an account of Sir Sidney Smith's brave defence of Acre against Buonaparte, whom he compelled to raise the siege.

"I wish that I had been there!" exclaimed Harry. "Captain Leslie says we ought to be afloat again, and it's right, I know, though home is very pleasant. We are sure, if we go, to obtain our promotion before long, and once lieutenants, if we have luck, we shall soon win our next step; till I get that, I feel too sure that I shall have no chance of gaining the object nearest my heart."

"What is that, Harry?" I asked.

"Perhaps I ought to have told you before, father; but the secret was not mine alone," was the answer.

Harry then told me what I suspected long ago, that he had set his heart on marrying Miss Fanny Leslie.

"I hope you have not told her so, my boy," I said; " the captain would not approve of it."

"Yes, father, I have though," he answered; "and she has promised to marry me if her parents will allow her.

"I am very sorry to hear this, for one thing, Harry," I said; "I fear it will cause you and her much disappointment and sorrow. The captain is very kind; he wishes you well, but he is proud of his family; and he will not allow his daughter to marry a man about whose birth he knows nothing, and who has no fortune. He will also be vexed to find that his daughter has engaged herself without first consulting him and her mother."

"But we have known each other from childhood, and he always encouraged me to come to the house," pleaded Harry; "and so Fanny thinks that he will not object to me."

"It's my belief he never thought such a thing possible," I observed; "I daresay he will blame himself when he finds it out, but that won't make him excuse you. I wish you would tell Miss Fanny what I say. The best thing you can now do is to set each other free; and if she remains unmarried, and you obtain your promotion and discover that you are of a family to which her father would not object, you can then come forward openly and claim her."

This, I am sure, was good advice.

"But, father, I cannot say this to Fanny; she would think me hard-hearted and that I did not really love her," said Harry.

"If she trusts you, and is a sensible girl, she will see that you are acting rightly," I answered. "Do what is right, and trust that all will come well in the end. That is a sound maxim, depend on it."

Harry at last replied that he would think over what I had said.

The next day he told me that he had spoken to Miss Fanny, who, though it made her very unhappy, had at last acknowledged that I was right, and consented to do as I had advised; assuring him, however, that she would never change. I was thankful to hear this, as it saved me from speaking to the captain, which I should have otherwise felt bound to do.

A few days after this I received orders to join the *Vestal* frigate; and though neither I nor they expected it, Reginald and Harry were appointed as master's mates to the same ship. I had to go on board at once, and they joined a few days afterwards. We were ordered to fit out with all despatch, and were quickly ready for sea.

I felt sorry at having to leave without again hearing from Jerry, for of course I could not tell what might happen to me; and there was nothing I more desired, for Harry's sake, than to find out who his parents had been. When I thought what a fine, handsome, gallant young fellow he was, I could not help hoping that he would have no reason to be ashamed of them. At all events, he would not be worse off than he was; and supposing that, after all, his birth was not such as he could boast of, he might still win a name for himself, as many another officer had done, who had, as the saying is, "gone in through the hawse-hole," just as the renowned Captain Cook and several of our bravest captains and admirals had done.

We had gone out to Spithead, and "Blue Peter" was flying from the fore, when who should come alongside in a boat from Ryde but Susan herself. I had bidden her good-bye, and did not expect to see her again.

"I have brought a letter," she said; "and as it is from Jerry, I did not like to trust it to anyone else."

She had just given it to me, when I received the order to "Pipe up anchor"; so all I could do was to shove it into my pocket, while Susan hurried down the side without knowing its contents. This was very trying to her, and I wished that she had looked at it before bringing it off.

When a ship is making sail, the boatswain has more to do than anybody else, and some hours passed before I could get to my cabin and break the seal; it was, as Susan supposed, from Jerry. Having it still by me, I give it in his own words :—

"DEAR OLD SHIP,—I am comfortably moored at last in a cottage of my own, with a small independence left me by my father—more than I deserved. I might have had it years ago, if my good sister Mary and her husband, Mr. Pengelley, had known where to find me. I had been here some time before I could make up my mind to let Mary know who I was. Instead of giving me the cold shoulder, bless her heart, she welcomed me at once, and I have been as happy as the day is long ever since, except when I think of the past and my own folly; but as it does me no good dwelling on that, I try to forget it. Mr. Pengelley is a lawyer, and lawyers, as you know, hear a good many things. One

8

day I told him about Harry; he had never heard of a child being saved from the wreck of the *Royal George*, nor had any people about here that I can make out. The next day he told me that he had been thinking over the matter, and asked me if I had ever in my wanderings been to the house of an old Mr. Hayward, living some miles off. I remembered not only the house, which is a very solitary one, half a mile or more from any highroad, but the old gentleman himself, and a lady whom I heard was his widowed daughter. She spoke to me kindly when I first went there, and said that she loved sailors, and wanted to hear all about the sea. She invited me into the house, and gave me a good dinner, and begged that I would look in whenever I came that way. I went several times. Though she was every inch a lady, I saw no servant in the house, and guessed that she took care of the old gentleman; indeed it was evident that their means were very scanty. She must have been very pretty in her youth, but care and sorrow had left their traces on her countenance; and I remembered, too, that she was always dressed in black. 'I will tell you her history,' said Mr. Pengelley. 'Her father, Mr. Hayward, was once a flourishing merchant at Bristol, and she, his only daughter, was looked upon as his heiress. A young naval officer, Henry Stafford, met her at Bath, where she was staying with some friends ; they fell in love with each other, and were engaged to marry as soon as he got his promotion, for he was then only a mate in the service. He and his only sister, Emily, lived with their widowed mother at the same place. Henry had good prospects, for he was heir to his uncle Sir Mostyn Stafford, of an old and very proud family, who had an estate in the neighbouring county. When the baronet heard that his nephew was about to marry without consulting him, he was very indignant, and declared that if he persisted in connecting himself with a family which he looked upon as inferior to his own, he would stop the allowance he now made him, and not leave him a penny beyond the title and estate, from which he could not cut him off. Henry did not believe that his uncle would, or indeed could, act as he threatened. He would possibly have, at all events, deferred his marriage ; but going one day to see Miss Hayward, he found her in great distress. She then told him that her father was on the point of failing, and wished her to marry a man of large means, who would help him out of his difficulties On this, Henry Stafford, fearing that he should lose her altogether, persuaded her to run off with him, promis-

ing to raise money, as he thought he could, to assist her
father. They married, and Henry, who was the idol of
his mother, took his young wife to live with her and
his sister. He soon discovered that he was utterly
unable to help Mr. Hayward as he intended; and
though the merchant was at first much annoyed at his
daughter's clandestine marriage, he was quickly recon-
ciled to her, especially when she told him of Harry's
intentions. He soon afterwards failed, when, without
making any attempt to retrieve his fortunes, he went
to live at the retired house where he still resides.
When Sir Mostyn Stafford heard that his nephew had
actually married, he was highly incensed, and carried
out his threats, depriving even Mrs. Stafford of a
portion of her income over which he had power. As
he was not a badly-disposed man, I believe that he
would not have acted thus severely towards his nephew
and sister-in-law had he not been greatly influenced by
a cousin of his, Biddulph Stafford, who was heir to the
estate after Henry. Biddulph Stafford's whole soul
was set on making money, and he had been heard to
express his satisfaction when war broke out, as Harry
was in the navy, that the enemy's shot might give him
possession of the estate and title. His vexation and
disappointment was therefore very great when young

Mrs. Stafford gave birth to a son, and from that moment he had redoubled his efforts to induce the baronet to take harsher measures towards his nephew. Harry was compelled to go to sea as the only means of finding support for his young wife and child. He had been afloat about a year or more, when Mr. Hayward fell ill, and his daughter hurried off to see him, leaving her child in charge of Mrs. Stafford and Emily. What Biddulph Stafford's object was I don't know, but, being well informed of all that occurred, he persuaded Sir Mostyn to offer not only to restore to Mrs. Stafford her income, but to increase it, provided she would consent not again to receive her daughter-in-law, and to bring up the child herself. This was a hard trial to the poor young mother, but she could not hold out when old Mrs. Stafford persuaded her son to consent to the arrangement under the belief that it was likely to prove advantageous to the boy. Both Mrs. Stafford and her daughter had, however, cause to regret this arrangement, for they found that they were constantly watched, they believed, by some agent of Biddulph, and they were persuaded his object was to get possession of the child; however, by constant vigilance, they were able to defeat it. Now comes the mysterious part of the business. Old Mrs. Stafford,

who had been for some time in declining health, died;
and the day after her funeral Emily and the child
disappeared. The idea was that either Biddulph had
won her over, or that she, frightened by his threats, had
gone off secretly to escape from him, thinking that by
some means or other he would get hold of the boy.
The latter opinion I believe to be the true one; indeed,
Biddulph Stafford, having been seen at Bath the day
before, it is possible that he might have followed Emily,
and by some means or other got possession of the child
—perhaps have carried the aunt and her nephew off
abroad. That there was foul play no one doubted.
Young Mrs. Stafford was as much in the dark as anyone; she had not heard from Emily, nor had she been
aware of her intention of leaving Bath. Living so
completely out of the world as she did, it was not till
some time after that she heard her child and sister-
in-law were missing. When the account of the loss of
the *Royal George* reached her, she knew that it was the
ship aboard which her husband was serving, and she
was for some days left in doubt whether he was among
the many who perished or the few which escaped. In
vain she waited to hear from him; at last she saw his
name among the list of those who were lost. It was
a wonder that she did not sink under her misfortunes,

and she would probably have done so had she not undertaken the sacred task of watching over her invalid father. Another strange circumstance occurred : Biddulph Stafford, who knew all along where she was living, unexpectedly called on her, and expressed the greatest sympathy with her at the loss of her husband, and offered to assist her in obtaining a portion of the subscriptions raised for the widows of those who perished. She, knowing less about him than her sister-in-law did, accepted his offer. He assured her also that he had made every inquiry for Emily and the little boy, but could not trace in what direction they had gone. It was remarkable that all the information she obtained about the wreck of the *Royal George* was from her cousin, and he seems thoroughly to have won her confidence by his apparently frank and pleasing manners.'

"Such was the account I received from Mr. Pengelley. I wish I could tell you more; but I cannot help thinking that something will come of it, and you may depend on me for doing my best to ferret out the truth, as I think you may also on my good brother-in-law. Good-bye for the present, Ben; I don't know whether it will be wise to tell this to your young friend."

I thought the matter over, and at last resolved to

make a copy of the letter, and to give it, sealed up, into Harry's keeping. I did so, charging him not to open it, except in the case of my death. Recollecting Susan's natural curiosity to know the contents of the letter, and also in case the original and the first copy should be lost, I made a second, which I sent on shore at Falmouth, charging Susan not to show it to anyone. I also wrote to Jerry, thanking him for his exertions, and begging him to send Susan all the information he could collect.

We had been at sea some time, and had taken a French privateer and three Spanish merchantmen, though we had met with no enemy which offered opposition. We were cruising in the Bay of Biscay, when one evening, Cape Ortegal bearing south-west, distant eight or nine leagues, we discovered a large fleet to windward, which our captain believed consisted of Spanish merchant vessels under convoy of some men-of-war.

"We will pick up some of those fellows before long," he exclaimed; and we stood towards the enemy. As we drew near we made out five frigates and two men-of-war brigs, with full eighty merchant vessels, steering to the northward, having apparently come from Cadiz. In spite of their number, our captain kept to his

resolution of attacking them, and stood on till we
weathered the leading frigate, which was ahead and
some distance from the convoy. The darkness of night
had come on when we got up alongside the enemy.
Our captain hailed and asked her name. The answer
was—

" The Spanish frigate *Ceres.*"

" Then strike your colours," cried our captain.

The enemy did not obey the order, and we immediately poured a broadside into her. The Spaniards
returned it, doing us little damage. While we were
loading our guns, to give her a second dose, she put
up her helm, and endeavoured to join her consorts to
leeward. We immediately kept away and engaged her
to leeward, and in about twenty minutes we had
silenced her fire, having had only a couple of men hit;
we were about to take possession, when we saw the
other four frigates close to us. While hauling up, to
avoid being raked by the leading frigate which had
opened her fire on us, we fell aboard her, carrying away
her maintopsail-yard. We had handled her pretty
roughly, when two more frigates coming up, one on
each side of us, we kept blazing away at both of them,
till the fourth arrived, followed by the two brigs. We
were now surrounded by more enemies than even our

fire-eating captain thought it prudent to contend with. However, either the Spaniards forgot to put shot in their guns, or fired them wildly, for we received but little damage, only two more men having been hit; we quickly hauled to the wind and stood out from among them, unharmed, although they were blazing away as fast as they could get their guns to bear on us. We then steered for a part of the convoy which had been somewhat scattered during the action, and succeeded in cutting off a large brig; but as the frigates were close upon our heels, we had only time to send a couple of boats on board, under the command of Harry and Mr. Leslie, who, having taken out her crew, set her on fire fore and aft. So rapidly had they executed their orders, that they were back again in a little more than five minutes, and we again made all sail, just as the four Spanish frigates coming up got us within range of their guns. As we had no longer any chance of capturing either of them, we continued our course, and soon ran them out of sight, they evidently having no inclination to follow us. Though it was not to be compared to our escape from Toulon, still it was a dashing piece of business, which required good seamanship to accomplish, and I therefore think it worthy of being mentioned.

Both Harry and Reginald were naturally anxious to do something to distinguish themselves, by which they might make sure of their promotion. They had behaved admirably on every occasion, and all they wanted was the opportunity which, as is well known, does not fall to the lot of every man.

We had been cruising in the northern part of the Bay of Biscay, when, standing towards Brest, we made out under the batteries in Camaret Bay a brig-of-war at anchor, with springs on her cable. One of our lieutenants was ill, and another away in a prize. Harry, to his great satisfaction, having got leave to lead an expedition to cut her out, asked for me to accompany him; Reginald had command of one boat, and a midshipman had charge of a third. We knew that there were several ships-of-war at anchor scarcely a mile off, which might have sent their boats to stop us if they had known what we were about. We stood inshore as soon as it was dark, and when about two miles from the place hove-to. The boats were lowered, and we shoved off. Harry and I were in the cutter, a fast-pulling boat, and kept ahead of the other two boats. We could tell the position of the brig by the lights on shore, and, after a hard pull, we caught sight of her. We guessed by the sounds that reached us that her crew were at quarters, but, though the other boats were still some way astern, Harry was eager to board at once; we made for her quarter, and hooking on, we sprang over her bulwarks with our cutlasses in hand. The Frenchmen made a desperate rush at us; I looked round, but nowhere could I see Harry. The next instant I found myself hurled back into the boat among several of our men who had boarded with me. I sang out for Harry, but he was not in the boat, and I feared that he had been cut down; just then I heard his voice, and found that he had sprung into a trawl-net which hung over the brig's quarter. We made another attempt to gain the deck, and kept back the Frenchmen; while Harry extricated himself, with the help of two of the men, from his dangerous position, and leapt back into the boat, into which we were again driven.

"Haul the boat more ahead, and we will try it again!" he shouted out.

Though I had had a thrust with a pike in my side, and I guessed that several other men were wounded, not being aware, however, that Harry himself had been hurt, we again sprang on board. I kept close to him this time, and warded off a heavy blow aimed at his head; pistols were flashed in our faces, pikes thrust at us, and cutlasses were whirled round our heads, and

HARRY AND BEN BOARDING THE FRENCH BRIG.

125

again we were driven back with more men hurt, while
I had received another wound from a cutlass. I began
to fear that we should not succeed. It was but for a
moment. Harry's voice cheered me up—

"At them again, lads!" he shouted; and once more
we sprang up the side, cutting down every one of the
Frenchmen within reach of our weapons. Six or eight
of us having gained the deck, the rest followed; and
charging the Frenchmen we drove them aft, killing or
wounding everyone who attempted to withstand us.
In less than three minutes the brig was ours, and the
enemy cried out for quarter, even before the other two
boats came up. The men in them not required at the
oars jumped on board to assist in securing the prisoners,
the cable was cut, and, while we were making sail, the
boats took the prize in tow; and before the people
in the forts knew what had happened, we were standing away from the land. We found that six Frenchmen had been killed, and twenty wounded, some of
them pretty badly. We had lost one man, and eight of
us were wounded, Harry in two places, and I in no less
than six. As soon as we got the breeze, we took the
boats in tow, and stood towards the frigate. The captain
was highly pleased at the success of the enterprise,
and told Harry that he might be sure of his promotion.

We had been on the point of returning home, and we now made the best of our way with our prize up Channel. I was not aware, till the doctor came to overhaul me, how much I had been hurt, and the next day I was unable to leave my cabin. Harry, who had the cabin of the absent lieutenant, was also confined to his. As soon as he could, he came to see me.

"I would willingly have been much more hurt rather than have missed taking the prize," he said, after he had inquired how I was getting on. "I hope that Captain Leslie will at least see that I am worth something."

"No doubt about that, Harry," I answered. "You did well, and I am proud of you; still be wise, and don't presume on what you have done."

I don't think Harry quite liked my advice; however, he said nothing. I think that Reginald must have been a little jealous of him, though it was not his fault that he had not been up in time to board the brig before we had possession of her; at all events, he did not show what he felt, and spoke as if he admired Harry more than ever.

As soon as we arrived at Spithead, Harry, Reginald, and I got leave to go on shore; Harry had by this time nearly recovered, but the doctor said that I must

not expect to be fit for duty for many weeks to come.
Reginald at once went home, and Harry accompanied
me. If nobody else was proud of him, Susan at all
events was, and I had good reason to be thankful that
I had such a wife to look after me. The same evening
Reginald came down and begged Harry to come to the
house, as his father and mother and all the ladies were
anxious to see him. Reginald had been giving a full
account of Harry's gallantry, and I suspect from what
Susan heard, that Miss Fanny had somewhat betrayed
her feelings. Harry came back in high spirits, accompanied by Reginald, to help him along; I was altogether
laid up, and, though Harry could not walk far, he managed
to get every day to the captain's house. In less than
ten days he received his commission as lieutenant.

"I knew you would!" I exclaimed as he held it up
proudly to me. "All you wanted was the opportunity,
and you got that."

"I hope that Reginald will get his too!" he exclaimed,
"for he deserves it, as he would have done the same
had he had the chance I got. I must go up to the
captain's, and tell them," he said.

"I was on the point of cautioning him about his
behaviour to Miss Fanny, but I had not the heart
just then to do it, he looked so proud and happy.

9

Off he went, and didn't come back till late in the evening, as he had been asked to stop and dine. Next day he had to go over to Portsmouth to order his uniform.

"I must go up and see Miss Fanny first," he said; "she told me that the captain spoke so highly of me that she is satisfied he would not object to our marriage. I shall have, as you know, a good share of prize-money, and we think that we shall have enough to keep house; so she was to tell the captain this morning, and we hope to have it all settled.

"I don't like to damp your spirits, Harry," I said, "but, my dear boy, don't be too sure; the captain could do nothing else than speak highly of your conduct; but that makes me think, as I have all along, that he never dreamt of his daughter and you falling in love with each other. However, you are bound to go up and hear what he has to say, and if he is not pleased, don't show any anger, but say that you will wait patiently till you have gained another step in rank, or have discovered who are your parents; and that if it should be proved that your family is not inferior to his, that you hope he will then withdraw any objections he may at present entertain."

"I trust that I shall not have to say that," answered Harry; "I would rather be accepted on my own merits."

"So you are by the young lady; and that is the chief matter. Parents are apt to look at things in a different light to young people," I observed.

Susan and I sat anxiously waiting Harry's return. I forgot to say that I had been hoping, day after day, to hear from Jerry, and had written telling him of Harry's gallantry, and that he and I were at home again. I had, however, received no answer. Harry had been absent fully three hours. I saw, as soon as he appeared, that all had not gone well. He threw himself into a chair. Susan waited for him to speak. At last she said, in her gentle way—

"I am afraid, dear Harry, that the captain does not see things in the light you expected."

"No, mother, he does not," he answered. "He spoke as if he wished to be as kind as possible, but what he said went to my heart.

"'I have regarded you with sincere affection, having known you from your childhood, and as the friend of my son,' he began; 'but I did not expect that you would have thus returned any service I may have rendered you. I have been wrong, I confess, to permit the intimacy which has existed between you and all the members of my family; but I tell you at once that I have an insuperable objection to any one of my daughters marrying a man whose family is unknown to me. For yourself I shall always entertain the truest regard, and I must beg you to receive this answer as final. Though Mrs. Leslie and I shall regret the loss of your society, you will see that, under the circumstances, it is better that you should not again come to my house.'

" I tried to argue the point, and spoke to the captain as you advised, father; but all I said had no effect, and showed me he had made up his mind how to act. He would not even allow me to see Fanny; and from being the happiest of human beings, I am now one of the most miserable."

Susan and I did what we could to comfort Harry, though without much avail. I was therefore thankful when the next day a letter from the Admiralty came appointing him as third lieutenant to the *Vestal*, and directing him to join at once. Reginald came down immediately afterwards, as he had also been ordered to join his ship; and he proposed that they should go over to Portsmouth that afternoon. Harry agreed ; and though Susan and I were sorry to lose him so suddenly, we saw that it was the best thing he could do.

A week afterwards the *Vestal* sailed down Channel, and, judging by Harry's last letter, I hoped that he had somewhat regained his spirits.

CHAPTER IX

I HAD been some time at home, and had pretty nearly recovered from my wounds. Susan frequently went up to see Jane; and the ladies treated her, notwithstanding what had occurred, as kindly as ever; but the captain ceased to inquire after me, and he evidently had not got over his annoyance, and still believed that Susan and I, if we had not encouraged Harry, might have at all events prevented him from falling in love with Miss Fanny. The poor young lady had not recovered her spirits; and Susan said she was afraid that if anything should happen to Harry it would bring her to her grave. This of course made us more than ever anxious to hear again from Jerry. At last one day the postman brought a letter to our door and demanded three shillings for it, which I willingly paid, for I saw at a glance that it was from my old shipmate. I have it still by me; here it is:—

"DEAR OLD SHIP,—What I told you in my last has prepared you for the news I have now to give. I thought over what Mr. Pengelley had told me, and could not help hoping that we should at last find out all about Harry St. George.

"The very first time that I saw Mrs. Stafford (though I did not know her name then) she told me that her husband had been an officer on board the *Royal George*, and that he was lost when the ship went down; but she said nothing more at that time. When, however, I heard that she had had a little boy who had disappeared with her young sister-in-law, I at once jumped to the conclusion that the young lady who had come to your house was Miss Stafford, and that the little boy was her nephew. It struck me that nothing was more likely than that Miss Stafford should have set off to see her brother, and consult with him what was best to be done for the safety of his son ; but, as you know, it's a very different matter to guess a thing and to prove it. Still I am almost as certain as I am of my own existence, that the little boy you saved from the wreck was Harry Stafford's son; but my thinking so won't get him his rights. Biddulph Stafford and I were young men together before I went off to sea, and many a wild prank we played; some of them such as I don't like to think about. There was an act of his, indeed, which, if known, would bring him under the power of the law; and I feel sure that if I were to introduce myself to him, and let him know that I was acquainted with it, and could bring witnesses to prove his guilt, long ago as it happened, I might gain an influence over him, which I might exercise for Harry's benefit. Sir Mostyn Stafford, you will understand, is still alive, and all Biddulph's scheming and plotting has hitherto gained him no advantage. My first idea was to go and give him his choice, either to acknowledge Harry, or to take the consequences of having his crime made known; he might, however, set me at defiance. The difficulty would be to prove that the young lady you saw was Miss Stafford, and then that the child saved from the wreck was the same little boy she had brought with her. The first thing to be done, as it seemed to me, was to learn from Mrs. Stafford if she knew how her little boy was likely to have been dressed; and if she described him as you had seen him, it would settle the matter in our minds, and we might possibly get Mr. Pengelley, or some other lawyer, to take up the case, and try to gain his rights for your young Harry. As soon as this idea occurred to me, I went back to Mr. Pengelley; he thought that I might be right, but told me to wait till he had obtained some more certain information as to how the Stafford estates were settled.

This took up some time, for lawyers seem to me to have a peculiarly slow way of setting about a business; probably they find from experience that 'Slow and steady wins the race.'   At last he sent for me, and told me that I might go off and see Mrs. Stafford, and gain all I could from her.   I of course lost not a moment. She recognised me at once, though she was naturally surprised to find how I was changed.   I introduced the subject cautiously.   I then asked her if she thought it possible that her son was still alive?   She said that sometimes she had hopes, but then she could not understand how it was that her sister-in-law had never written to her.   At last I asked her if she could describe what her son was like?   'Yes,' she said, 'for I have his portrait, which Emily sent me a few days only before her mother's death.'   'Will you allow me to see it?' I asked; and going to her room she returned with a small well-done drawing of a little boy, exactly like what Harry might have been, and dressed as you described him, in a sailor's jacket and trousers and round hat.

"'You see him in a dress I made for him myself, and sent only a short time before.   I also made a copy of it, which I forwarded to my poor husband on board the *Royal George.*'

"'Did it ever occur to you, ma'm,' I asked, 'that

your sister may have gone to see her brother on board the *Royal George*, and taken the little boy with her?'

"'Yes, indeed,' she answered, 'I thought that possible; but when I heard that all the women and children on board had perished, I knew that if such were the case, both Emily and my child must have been lost also.'

"'Did you ever hear, ma'm, that a little boy was saved from the wreck?' I said.

"'No,' she answered. 'Mr. Biddulph Stafford, who kindly came here at the time, and told me all about it, did not mention that any child was saved; but oh! say, was such really the case? Could my boy have been on board and escaped the fate which overtook his father?'

"I thought it time to describe to the poor mother how a young lady came with a little boy, exactly like the picture she had just shown me, to your cottage, and how you had saved the same child after the ship had gone down, and that the same boy was now an officer in the navy.

"'Oh, merciful Providence, he must be my own boy! I should know him even now, he cannot be so changed,' she exclaimed.

"I told her, though I did not wish to raise her hopes to disappoint them, that I felt sure she was right. But

then I suggested that though she might be confident
that Harry St. George was her son, it might be very
difficult to prove it so as to enable him to obtain his
rights.

" ' If we could prove that Miss Stafford went to Ryde
with her nephew, it would greatly assist the case,' I
observed.

" ' I will look over all her letters to me, and see if
she ever mentioned that she thought of so doing,' she
said. 'I have some also which my husband wrote to
her during their mother's illness, and he may possibly
have expressed a wish to see her and our boy. But
surely, even should I not discover anything of the sort,
Sir Mostyn Stafford will be convinced that my son is
his nephew, and would not refuse to acknowledge him.'

" About that, I said, I could not be sure ; but I
advised her not on any account to let Mr. Biddulph
Stafford know that she had gained tidings of her son,
lest he might influence Sir Mostyn. I told her that
I was sure my brother-in-law, Mr. Pengelley, would,
with the evidence she was able to bring forward, undertake her case ; and I offered, should Harry St. George be
in England, to go to Ryde and bring him back with me.

" ' I am indeed most grateful,' she answered. ' I
must not leave my poor father, or I would go myself to

see my son, for that he is my boy I have not a doubt on my mind.'

"Just as I was about to leave the room, my eye fell on a small portrait of a lady hanging against the wall, and it occurred to me that it might be that of Miss Stafford. I asked the question. Mrs. Stafford said it was; and I proposed taking it with me to know whether you and your wife could recognise it, and perhaps others might be found who may have seen her on board the *Royal George* to do so likewise.

"She at once took down the portrait, which with that of her son she carefully packed up and entrusted to my care. After again cautioning her against Mr. Biddulph Stafford, I wished her good-bye, and returned with the information I had gained to my worthy brother-in-law, who, on hearing it, said that he was convinced in his own mind that Harry St. George was the son of Henry Stafford, and that he would undertake his case, though he advised me to caution you and him not to be too sanguine about gaining it; at the same time you might be sure that Mrs. Stafford would acknowledge him, and that he would thus, which he would probably value more than fortune, be able in the eyes of his friends to establish his right to bear his father's name.

"Mr. Pengelley hopes that you will on no account let anyone learn the history I have now given you till everything is prepared.   Should Biddulph Stafford hear that young Harry is discovered, he will stir heaven and earth to prevent him from establishing his rights.   I might, as I before said, by threatening to expose the crime of his early days, gain a power over him; but as it occurred so long ago, he might feel himself safe and set me at defiance.   At all events be cautious, and let no one but Harry and your wife, who, from what I saw of her, is, I should judge, a discreet woman, know anything of the matter."

This letter, as may be supposed, threw Susan and me into a great state of agitation.   We could talk of nothing else, and kept looking out every moment for Jerry's arrival; we could not help grieving that Harry was not at home, for we could take no steps without him.   We were sorry, too, that we could not consult with Captain Leslie, as Jerry had forbidden us to speak to anyone on the subject.   He, I was sure, could be trusted, though he had been so much offended with Harry for venturing to look up to Miss Fanny; but the state of the case was now greatly altered; and should Harry be able to prove that he was heir to Sir

Mostyn Stafford, instead of being without name or family, I knew of course that the captain would no longer think of forbidding him to marry his daughter.

I had one day walked down to the beach, when a wherry from Portsmouth came to an anchor, and soon after a boat reached the shore with several people in her. Among them was a one-legged man, with white hair, who looked to my eyes like an old post-captain or admiral. I went up to him, at first with some doubt in my mind, but soon saw that it was no other than my old shipmate Jerry.

He put out his hand and shook mine cordially, saying as he did so, "You are less changed than I am, Ben, but years make a difference in a man. Stay, I must not lose sight of my valise. Once upon a time I should have made nothing of carrying it myself, but I am not as strong on my pins as I used to be. Can you get someone to take it up to your house? We will keep him in sight, however; because, as you may guess, I should not like to lose it."

I said that I would carry it myself, and, taking it out of the boat, shouldered it and walked up alongside Jerry, who stumped along with much less briskness than formerly; indeed I saw that he was greatly aged since we last met. On reaching home, after Susan had welcomed him, he caught her eye turned towards the valise.

"You are anxious to see the portraits I wrote about," he observed, getting up and opening it. The first he took out was that of the little boy.

"That's like him all over," exclaimed Susan. "I should have known it even if I had not expected to see it; and it's just the same as the one I have upstairs, though that is terribly faded."

"Please get it, Mrs. Truscott, and we will compare the two," said Jerry. She quickly brought the little picture we had so carefully preserved; though the colours were almost gone, the lines were sufficiently clear to remove any manner of doubt in our minds that the one was a copy of the other.

"And now, what do you think of this?" producing a portrait of Miss Stafford.

"The very young lady who came to our house," exclaimed Susan. "Owing to the sad circumstances of her death, her features are more impressed on my mind than those of anyone I ever met, and I am sure those who know Harry would say that he is wonderfully like her."

I agreed with my wife, and Jerry said that he thought so likewise from what he recollected of him; indeed we had not a shadow of doubt on our minds that our dear Harry was the son of Henry Stafford.

"Oh, how I wish he was at home!" cried Susan; "he cannot fail to gain his rights; and then he might marry dear Miss Fanny and be so happy. Ben, I must go and tell her what we have found out about his family, and that she may be sure all will come right. It will do her all the good in the world, for she has been very sadly since her father forbid Harry to come to the house and got him sent off to sea; sometimes I have thought that the poor dear would break her heart."

I asked Jerry what he thought.

"There might be no harm in letting Miss Fanny know, but it must depend upon whether she has got discretion or not," said Jerry. "If she is a wise girl she will hold her tongue, and I daresay it will make her happier to hear what you wish to tell her."

Susan at length gained her way, and, promising duly to caution Miss Fanny to be prudent, set off.

Jerry and I sat talking over matters till Susan came back.

"I am thankful I went," she said. "I found Miss Fanny very ill, and I have hopes that the news I gave her will restore her to health faster than any doctor's stuff."

I told Jerry how I had hunted for the young lady's

luggage, and had been unable to find it, though she had told me the name of the inn where she had left it; and I was sure she would not have spoken falsely.

" Is the landlord still alive ? " asked Jerry.

" Yes; though well in years," I answered.

" Well, then, we will go along together, and see if we can make anything out of him," said Jerry; and off we set. We went into the bar-room. Fortunately no one was there, so we asked the landlord to come in and have a quiet glass with a couple of old salts. He, nothing loath, came at once, for he had been a sailor himself. I never saw anybody like Jerry for leading on to a point he wanted to reach; he soon got talking about the *Royal George*, then he asked the landlord " if he remembered the name of the young lady who came to his house the day before the wreck with a little boy ? "

" No," said the landlord, "I don't remember her name, though I do her and the little boy."

" Then you heard it ? " said Jerry.

" Can't say but what I did," answered the landlord.

" Then can you tell me what the gentleman did with her luggage ? " he asked, looking the landlord full in the face. " Come, you know he bribed you to stow it away, and say nothing about it if questions were asked."

I never saw anybody look so astonished as the landlord did when Jerry said this.

"How should you know anything about it?" he asked.

"I know a good many things," answered Jerry, with a knowing look. "Come, mate, tell us what Mr. Biddulph Stafford paid you for stowing the things away, and I will promise that it shall be doubled if you can find them."

I did not know at the time that this was all a guess of Jerry's, but he had hit the right nail on the head.

"Is it a bargain?" asked the landlord. "I suppose that Mr. Biddulph can't do me any harm?"

"It's a bargain, and I will see that you are not the sufferer," said Jerry. "Come, what did he give you?"

"Ten pounds," answered the landlord.

"You shall have twenty; and that you may be sure of it, I will write out the promise to pay you."

The landlord, thus taken by surprise, agreed; and Jerry, who followed the wise plan of "striking while the iron is hot," made him then and there bring pen and paper, when he wrote out an order on his brother-in-law for twenty pounds. The landlord then begged that we would come upstairs, and, going through a trap-door in the roof, he let down two small trunks, such as ladies might use for travelling. They were both locked.

10

"There they are," said the landlord; "and the sooner you take them the better. They have made me uncomfortable ever since they have been in the house; I didn't like to destroy them, and I didn't know where to put them. As it is so long since Mr. Biddulph Stafford came here, I don't suppose that he will trouble me again about them."

We waited till dark, and the landlord then getting us a boy to carry one of the trunks, I shouldered the other, and we set off back to my house.

Though Susan was naturally curious to see their contents, we agreed that we would not open them ourselves, but wait till Mrs. Stafford could do so, as she was more likely than anyone else to recognise their contents. We then talked over what was best to be done. I was for telling Captain Leslie, for I was sure that he had still as kind a feeling towards Harry as ever, and that he had acted as he had done to prevent him and his daughter from making what he considered an imprudent match. Jerry at last came to agree with me, and he consented to write to Mr. Pengelley and ask his advice. Mr. Pengelley thought as I did, that as an old friend of Harry's the captain might be trusted; indeed, without his assistance it would have been difficult to get Harry sent home. I lost no time in hastening up to the captain, and told him everything; he was, as I expected he would be, highly delighted.

"He is a noble young fellow, and I all along thought he was of gentle birth, though he might not have a right to his father's name," he exclaimed. "We will get him home without delay, for of course nothing can be done till he arrives."

He promised to be cautious, so that Mr. Biddulph Stafford should not get an inkling of what we were about.

"I will accompany him myself and give him all the support in my power, as the whole matter is as clear to me as noonday, and, whether his uncle acknowledges him or not, he must win his case."

I told him that Jerry hoped he would not say anything to the rest of his family.

"I will be discreet," he answered, "depend upon that."

I had a strong suspicion that the ladies soon knew all about it, though for my part I was sure they would act wisely.

Jerry received a letter from Mr. Pengelley, saying that he wished to see him, and to bring the information he had gained. Bidding us, therefore, good-bye, he set off to return home, taking the portraits of the young lady and Harry with him.

After this there seemed nothing to be done but to
wait till Harry's return; Captain Leslie had written to
request that he might be allowed to come home on
urgent family affairs, and there was no doubt but that
he would obtain leave to do so, and he would of course
guess the object.

I spent a good part of each day with spyglass in
hand, looking out for fresh arrivals at Spithead. When
either Susan or I went up to the captain's, we were
sure to find Miss Fanny at the telescope, which stood
on a stand in the bay window of the drawing-room,
turned in the same direction. At last one day I saw
two frigates coming in round St. Helen's; the leading
one had her fore-topmast shot away and her sails and
rigging much cut up; the second, which had the
English colours flying over the French, was in a far
worse condition, her mainmast and mizzen-topmast
were gone, and her hull was severely battered. She
was evidently a prize to the first.

"I can't help hoping that yonder frigate is the
Vestal; it's hard to say positively, but she is, as far
as I can judge from this distance, wonderfully like her,"
I exclaimed to Susan. I hurried down to the "hard,"
and, engaging a boat, put off and got alongside before
any of the Portsmouth boats. I soon found that I was

right. The first person I saw on stepping on deck was
Harry himself; he hurried forward to shake me by the
hand.

"Father," he said, "we have had a glorious fight, and
the captain has been good enough to speak highly of
me; after an hour's fighting, broadside to broadside, we
got foul of the enemy, and I had the honour of leading
the boarders."

I asked him if he had received Captain Leslie's letter;
he had not.

"I am then the first to bring you the good news," I
said; and I told him in as few words as I could how
Jerry had discovered who his parents were, and that he
might before long see one of them. He was naturally
eager to go on shore at once, but he could not desert his
duty; so, sending the boat back with a message to
Susan, I remained on board till the frigate with her
prize went into harbour. Reginald was as much rejoiced
at his friend's prospects as Harry was himself. As soon
as they could get leave they accompanied me over to
Ryde.

We landed at the very spot where, about twenty
years before, I had stepped on shore with Harry in my
arms, all wet and draggled, followed by the sheep which
had saved his life. And now he stood by my side, a

fine, well-dressed young man, with the thorough cut of a naval officer. He had had time to get rigged out in a new uniform, and looked handsomer, I thought, than ever. Somebody else would think so, too, I had a notion.

We hurried up to our cottage, where Susan was on the lookout for him. He took her in his arms and kissed her, just as he would have done before he went to sea.

"Mother," he said, "you are looking well, and thankful I am to come back to you."

"You've another mother now, Harry," she said, gazing in his face, and the tears fell from her eyes.

"I shall not love you the less," he answered, "though I had a dozen mothers."

"There are more than her to share your love, Harry," she replied.

"Well, mother," he said, smiling, "I hope my heart is large enough for all."

"That it is, I am sure, Harry," she answered; "and I'll not grudge what you give to others."

Reginald had stayed outside the garden; when I looked out, I found that he had gone off home. Harry cast a wistful glance in the same direction; still he did not like to leave Susan in a hurry. She guessed what was passing in his mind.

"I mustn't be keeping you here, Harry," she said, "so do you go after Mr. Reginald. Miss Fanny will be looking for you, and she won't thank me if I keep you here. Now go, Harry, and bless you—bless you; my heart's very happy at seeing you back, for I'm sure that all will turn out as we wish it at last. You've had a sore trial, but you acted rightly."

Harry, having given Susan another embrace and shaken me warmly by the hand, bounded away after Reginald. I didn't offer to accompany him, for, in truth, I could not have moved as fast as he did; but I followed at my leisure, as the captain had told Susan he wanted to see me as soon as I came on shore. As I got near the house, I caught sight of Harry and Miss Fanny in the shrubbery, and from what I saw he had no reason to doubt that she loved him as much as ever; and I am sure that she would not have met him as she did, unless she had had the captain's leave to receive him as her intended husband. Mr. Reginald reached the house, and got through the greetings with the captain and his mother, and other sisters. A very happy party they looked, for he had a good account to give of himself, though maybe he hadn't quite as much to boast of as had Harry. From the way Harry was received when he at last made his appearance with Miss Fanny by his side, I felt sure that all was right.

I had afterwards a long talk with the captain. He told me that he was ready for a start as soon as Harry was at liberty. There was no time to be lost, for we could not tell what tricks Mr. Biddulph Stafford might be playing in the meantime. As far as we knew, he had as yet no inkling of what had occurred; but he was deep and cunning, according to Jerry's account, and would move heaven and earth, if his suspicions were aroused, to defeat our object. Some days, however, must pass before we could begin our journey, as Harry could not quit his ship till she was paid off. It was a question with us whether Mr. Biddulph Stafford knew that his nephew had been saved when the ship went down, or had found out the name we had given him; if he did, he would soon learn that he had come home again, and might possibly be on the lookout for him, thinking, of course, that Harry was still ignorant of who he really was. This idea came into the captain's head. He said that he thought it would be well to tell Harry, that he might be on his guard against any treacherous trick his uncle might endeavour to play him. I had not many fears on the subject; still I agreed that it would be better to be on the safe side.

Harry and Reginald spent that night on shore, and the next day returned to Portsmouth. It was on the evening of that day, as I happened to be passing the inn where Miss Stafford had left her boxes, when I caught sight of a strange gentleman coming along the road, and looking about him as if in search of some house or other. As I passed close to him I looked in his face, and could not help fancying that he was very like Harry, only much older, with a very different expression of countenance. After I had passed him I turned round, when I saw him looking up at the sign of the inn, and then go without further hesitation up to the door. I walked on some little way, and stood watching the inn till he came out again. As I again passed him I felt sure that he was no other than Mr. Biddulph Stafford, from the dark and troubled look I saw on his countenance. He then went on into the town. As the wind was from the north-east, and the tide was ebbing, I knew that no wherry was likely to put off for some time to come, and that I should be able to fall in with him again before he left the island. I accordingly entered the inn to learn what I could from the landlord. He presently, taking me into his private room, confessed that the stranger was no other than the man I suspected. He had at once made himself known, and asked what had become of the young lady's trunks, and seemed anxious to have them. The landlord at once told him that he could not give them, seeing that they were no longer in his possession, and that, for what he knew to the contrary, they had long since been destroyed. At last, when he pressed him, he told him that he had given them to two sailors to carry off into the middle of the Channel and sink them, thinking that was the best way of disposing of them. This seemed to satisfy him, and giving the landlord a guinea, and telling him not to say anything about the matter, he went off.

"That was not the truth, my friend," I observed.

"It was partly true," answered the landlord, "for you and the old gentleman who came with you were seamen—I could swear to that; and how should I know that you didn't sink them away there 'twixt this and Portsmouth?"

I had no time to argue the point with the landlord, though of course he was wrong, as I had to look after Mr. Biddulph Stafford. I found him on the shore, trying to engage a wherry to carry him across to Portsmouth; but none of the men would go, as it was blowing harder than ever, with a nasty sea running. At last I heard him offer five guineas to anyone who would cross. I knew by this that he must be in a desperate hurry.

"If you'll wait half an hour, sir, I'll do it," said the owner of a large wherry, coming up to him; we shall get across just as soon as we should if we were to start now."

To this Mr. Biddulph Stafford agreed, and I saw him go into an inn near the beach, to get some refreshment I suppose, telling the man to call him when he was ready. I now knew that I should have no difficulty in ascertaining whether he had really gone, so I hastened back to the captain, to tell him what I had discovered. He immediately wrote to Harry, to tell him to get ready for a start, and to meet himself and me at "The George," where we would call for him next morning, if we could get across, on our way to Mr. Pengelley's; adding, that the sooner we could get him recognised by his mother and uncle the better, lest Mr. Biddulph Stafford should be taking steps to defeat us. The letter was sent off by the mail-packet that night.

The captain agreed that it would be better that Susan should accompany us, as her evidence was sure to be wanted; so, calling at our cottage on my way back to the shore, I told her to pack up her traps and get a woman to take care of the house during her absence. Though she didn't like leaving home, she was willing to do anything for Harry's good, and promised to be ready in time.

On returning to the beach I found that Mr. Biddulph Stafford had just put off from the shore, but, with the wetting and tossing he would get, I felt pretty sure he wouldn't be ready to start till the next morning, if even then.

I daresay Miss Fanny would rather have had Harry come back at once to Ryde, but she was too wise to say anything about the matter. The next morning was fine, and the captain, Susan, and I crossed to Portsmouth, taking with us Miss Stafford's trunks, which I had had done up in canvas, and painted in such a way that even should Mr. Biddulph Stafford get sight of them they might not be recognised by him. We found Harry waiting for us at "The George." The ship had been paid off the previous day, and he and Reginald were now free. The latter went back to Ryde "to console Miss Fanny," as he said.

On making inquiries I found that Mr. Biddulph Stafford was sleeping at the hotel, and had not yet come out of his room, which convinced me that he had been knocked up the previous day by sea-sickness, and also that he did not know that we were trying to get ahead of him. The postchaise being ordered, we at once started, and, travelling as fast as the horses could get along, without any accident reached Mr. Pengelley's. Harry was of course very anxious to see his mother; and accordingly, leaving Captain Leslie with Mr. Pengelley, he and Jerry, with Susan and I, set off for the old house where she and her father lived. Mr. Pengelley, Jerry told us, had already somewhat prepared her for the recovery of her son.

As we approached the house we saw in the garden a fair lady dressed in black, who, though thin and care-worn, was still very handsome, attending to an old gentleman seated under a tree in an arm-chair. I guessed at once she must be Mrs. Stafford. Harry, who had been on the box, got down, while Jerry stumped forward, as fast as his wooden leg would let him, to announce us. He had scarcely begun to speak when the lady, fixing her eyes on Harry, rushed forward.

"You are indeed my son!" she exclaimed, as Harry supported her in his arms—for, as may be supposed, she was well-nigh overcome with agitation. However, it is more than I can do to describe all the particulars of the meeting. Harry was also not a little agitated, but, after some time, both he and Mrs. Stafford became calm, and she then led him forward towards the old gentleman in the chair, who was, as I of course knew, her father, Mr. Hayward. He glanced up at Harry, with a look of astonishment in his countenance.

"Why," he said, "I thought he had been drowned long, long ago!"

It was evident that he took Harry for his father. It satisfied me that Harry must be very like him. That he was so was further proved when Mrs. Stafford produced a miniature of her husband, which might have been that of Harry—though, according to Susan's notion, it was not so handsome. In the trunks, which Mrs. Stafford opened in our presence, she recognised, with many a sigh, various articles, and among them another miniature was discovered still more resembling Harry. When Mrs. Stafford heard who Susan was, she embraced her as if she were her sister, and the tears fell down from her eyes as she thanked her over and over again for her loving treatment of Harry.

We left Harry with his mother, and returned to the house of Mr. Pengelley, who, with Captain Leslie, had been busy in collecting such other evidence as was thought necessary. The next day Mr. Pengelley went

for Harry, and took him and his mother to see Sir
Mostyn Stafford, whose intellects, though he was an
old man, were still perfectly clear. On Harry being
introduced to him, after regarding him fixedly for a few
minutes he exclaimed, "There stands my nephew;
had I not been told that he was Henry's son, I should
have known him instantly."

Mr. Pengelley asked if he was ready to acknowledge
him; he replied that he should certainly do so. It
appeared that he had been for some time suspicious of
Mr. Biddulph Stafford, and was very glad to find an
heir who was likely to do more credit than that person
to his name and title.

I have already spun my yarn to a greater length
than I intended. I know nothing of the law, and
therefore cannot describe the legal proceedings which
took place; but all I know is, that the evidence we
brought forward was so overwhelming that Mr. Biddulph Stafford was defeated, and that Harry fully
established his claim as heir to Sir Mostyn Stafford.

As may be supposed, Captain Leslie no longer
objecting, Harry shortly afterwards married Miss
Fanny. A few weeks more passed, when, old Mr.
Hayward dying, Mrs. Stafford came to live with her
son, who, before a year was over, by the death of his

uncle, succeeded to the estate and title. No one was more pleased than Jerry with the result of his exertions. It seemed as if his last task had been accomplished; he was suddenly taken ill, and, though he lingered for some weeks, he gradually sank. Whatever the sins and failings of his youth, he had sincerely mourned for them, and now, enjoying the strong hope of a true Christian, he died. Harry and I followed the old man to his grave; Susan, who had been summoned to give evidence at the trial, returned with me after some time to Ryde, where we have since lived on, having seen another long war brought to a glorious conclusion.

One of my chief amusements is to describe to the members of another generation the battles I have seen fought, the adventures I have gone through, and, what I find interests them more than anything else, to repeat the account I have given in this book of "The Loss of the *Royal George*."

Printed by MORRISON & GIBB LIMITED, *Edinburgh*